The
Clemenceau Case

The
Clemenceau Case

Alexandre Dumas, fils

MINT EDITIONS

The Clemenceau Case was first published in 1866.

This edition published by Mint Editions 2021.

ISBN 9781513291321 | E-ISBN 9781513294179

Published by Mint Editions®

MINT
EDITIONS
minteditionbooks.com

Publishing Director: Jennifer Newens
Design & Production: Rachel Lopez Metzger
Project Manager: Micaela Clark
Translator: William Fléron
Typesetting: Westchester Publishing Services

To M. Rollinet, *Counselor-at-Law*

At the first news of my arrest, and without inquiring how much truth there was in the contradictory rumors circulated concerning me, you remembered our friendly relations, and persuaded me to live as long as possible for the sake of my child and my honor. I therefore now begin, not merely an account of the facts, the knowledge of which is indispensable to the counsel, who is willing to conduct my case, but also a confidential, exact, inexorable recital of the events, the circumstances, the thoughts which led up to the catastrophe of last month.

As the trial will come off no sooner than in five or six weeks, I shall have time to reflect. I will tell you the truth, as I would tell it to God, were he to question me, wishing to make my fate depend upon the sincerity of my confession. From this account you will take everything you may deem needful for my defence. I will give it as much continuity and clearness, as the state of my mind, less troubled than I should have expected, will allow. Your talent and friendship will do the rest.

Whatever the verdict of the jury may be, I shall never forget how you greeted me with open arms, when the door of my prison was opened to you; and my last thought, whether I be condemned or not, will be divided between my son and you.

Pierre Clemenceau
May 8th, 188—

Contents

I

I am of a family which is more than obscure. The words "my family" require explanation. My family was my mother. From her I received everything I have, my birth, my education, my name; for even now I do not know my father. If he is still alive, he will, like everybody else, have read in the daily papers the account of my arrest, and rejoice that he did not recognize a child who would one day have dragged his name into the criminal courts.

Very well. Up to the age of ten, I went pretty regularly to a little day school kept by an old man, on the ground floor of the house adjoining ours. There I learned reading, writing, and a little arithmetic, sacred history, and catechism.

When I had reached that age, my mother, sacrificing her own present happiness to my future good, placed me in a boarding school. It was hard for her to part with me; but, after commending me particularly to the care of the principal, telling him over and over again that he was to be gentle with me as I had never been away from her, she left me in his charge.

I pass over the disputes, the fights, and thousand and one petty annoyances to which a new boy is subjected in a boarding school, especially if that boy happens to be poor, and all the others rich, as in my case. My troubles were increased greatly because of the knowledge the others had of my being an illegitimate child. My mother had already warned me that that fact would cause me to be despised and insulted by many. I found, however, some compensation in the kindness of the teacher, who took special interest in my progress.

One day, when my school-mates were particularly exasperating, calling me "the bastard of Orleans," one of them, Constantin Ritz, interfered in my behalf.

In consequence of this incident, a warm friendship sprang up between Constantin and myself, which, among other things, led to my being invited to his home for the vacations.

Constantin's father, Thomas Ritz, had in his younger days shown great talent as a sculptor, and produced a fine statue which is now at the Luxemburg. From that effort he had gained great renown. But a rich young lady fell in love with him at the beginning of his career, and became his wife. Perhaps, by bringing too much comfort into their home, she had frightened away inspiration.

Thomas Ritz would have liked very much to see his son take to sculpture, for he felt himself capable of directing and instructing him in the great principles of art, in fact making him a true artist. Unfortunately, Constantin had no taste either for sculpture, music, or painting; he was, therefore, far from being of the same mind as his father, who, however, did not force his inclination, but allowed him to prepare for the military school of Saint Cyr.

One Sunday, M. Ritz, now a widower with but two children, Constantin and a daughter about sixteen years old, took me into his studio, where I saw so many plaster casts, marble, and bronze statues in all sorts of attitudes, solemn, affected, dramatic, that it fairly took my breath away. M. Ritz asked me which of all these statues I preferred, and when I pointed to a certain bronze figure, he told me I had shown great taste, for that was a copy of one of the finest works of antiquity— *the Wrestler*. "And," added he, smiling, "you are quite right, it is better than the others—which are my own."

I became at once a favorite with the old artist. That same evening, he asked me whether I had any ambition to become a sculptor, and proposed to have me remain at his house, where I should be treated as one of his own children.

I was now fourteen years old, and the resources of my mother had become inadequate to the strain of keeping me at school. Having had an opportunity to speak to her during the day, I told M. Ritz I should like it very much. Two days after, he and my mother decided that at the summer vacation I should leave school and take up my abode with him, which I accordingly did.

My progress was rapid; I loved work; I was indefatigable, rising early, staying up late, visiting museums and art galleries. I was ambitious; I wanted to leave something to posterity.

My mother was delighted; M. Ritz was proud of me. He showed my work to his artist friends. From them I received encouragement, counsel, sincere compliments.

I had, however, done nothing as yet but copy antique statues or follow my own fancy.

One evening, while his daughter was playing the piano, M. Ritz addressed me suddenly:

"Tomorrow you shall mould from nature. I am anxious to see what sort of a hand you will make at it. Prepare your clay the first thing in the morning. The model will arrive early."

"What model?" I asked with a palpitating heart caused by this important news; "man or woman?"

"A woman."

"Standing up or lying down?"

"Standing up."

My heart was literally bounding. I slept but little that night. The next morning by seven o'clock I was mixing my clay. M. Ritz entered.

"Are you in good form?" said he.

"Yes," I replied with assurance.

"Then let us breakfast.'

II

E xactly as the clock struck nine, there came a gentle knock at the studio door.

It was the model.

She was a person of from twenty to twenty-two years of age, in a dress of blue merino, quite short, and a straw hat trimmed with violet ribbons. A neat little collar, black and gray turban, plaid shawl, laced shoes, and silk gloves, much worn at the finger tips, completed her costume, which did not surprise me in the least, as I hardly supposed that a model at six francs a sitting, would be clad in velvet and lace; and besides, I had always been accustomed to see women plainly dressed among my mother's assistants, as well as my mother herself. The impression her dress gave me, was respect for the wearer, but it looked so plain upon the person of Mariette, that I asked myself by what miracle a Venus could come out of it.

There was nothing remarkable about her head, the eyes were soft, the hair auburn, the complexion ruddy, the teeth well enough, the nose flat, nothing fine about the profile, and her voice was pleasant. I need not tell you that M. Ritz treated his models with the greatest gentleness, and with perfect politeness.

"You have a cold, my dear child," he said to the young woman, as she coughed a little.

"It is nothing. I caught cold at M. P.'s. He is always too warm, and let the fire go out. Being dressed, he did not notice it."

"What is he doing now?"

"I don't know."

"Did you not look?"

"No, he does not like to have any one look at his pictures; all I know is, that I am posing on my knees with my arms lifted, and with an expression of terror. Perhaps it is another 'Lion de Florence.'"

I could hardly refrain from laughing.

"Well, never mind," said M. Ritz, "today you won't have to hold up your arms."

"It's all the same to me, it's so nice and warm here."

"Very well, let us begin."

Mlle. Mariette moved away from the stove, near which she had stood since she came in. I tried to assume a careless attitude, but I was very nervous within.

Taking off her shawl and hat, she stepped upon the platform, saying to M. Ritz:

"Everything?"

"Yes."

In the most simple manner in the world, as if it were a perfectly natural thing to do, the girl unhooked her waist, unbuttoned her cuffs, slipped off her dress and, picking it up, placed it on a chair; removing the collar, she carefully laid it aside, and untying the skirt, stood clad only in a chemise, as she wore no corset. She sat down, throwing the right leg over the left, and unlaced her gaiters in a similar pose to that which Pradier has given one of his most beautiful statuettes; then she drew off her stockings, and dropping her chemise, pushed it aside with her bare foot, and rising, threw her head back, lifting with both hands the hair which rested on her shoulder.

"How am I to pose?" she asked. I turned toward M. Ritz, as much to regain my composure, as to get his idea. Stretched upon the sofa, he had not taken his eyes from me for several minutes. "Choose your pose," he said to me.

"Just as mademoiselle has taken it;" I replied, in an unsteady voice.

"Very well;" he nodded.

But Mariette had let her arms fall. I said to her, "Lift your hair again, mademoiselle, as you did a moment ago."

She repeated the gesture, but with less happy effect.

"Throw your head back a little more, not so, but so." And, without thinking of what I was doing, I jumped upon the platform, and taking her by the wrists, replaced her exactly in the pose which I wished to reproduce.

"So it seems," she said, with a smile, "that I am always to have my arms lifted."

Taking off my vest, I turned back my sleeves, raised the seat of my stool until it was on a level with my work, and courageously attacked the lump of clay.

"I am going to work too," said M. Ritz as he went to his studio; "don't let the fire go out."

Strange enough, my mind repeated all other thoughts, except that of reproducing what I saw.

In a moment everything seemed to be entirely normal. I undertook to represent my living model, as I had always tried to represent my inanimate figures; but more than this, I was now impatient to catch the life-like expression, and to at once embody an impression which might escape me a moment later. The ardor with which I worked was thus stimulated by a struggle to capture a reality. There was mingled with it, also, an admiration for that body, which I contemplated for the first time; an admiration entirely devoid of any sensual ideas.

How far below nature are the most beautiful creations of art! I realized now a remark, which I had often heard from my master and his friends: "Nature is so discouraging." And in this manner, I explained to my own satisfaction, why it was that so many artists hold fast to tradition, and prefer to copy the works of men, rather than to address themselves directly to the work of God.

In regard to proportion, there are indeed certain statues more perfect than any woman, and, if God, accepting thus the co-operation of a mortal, should see fit to animate one of these masterpieces, she would be, I believe, more perfect than any of the most famous beauties, embracing in her person all the genius of art together with the best gifts of the Creator. But God need not perform this pagan miracle, for the most incomplete of His works remains, and will remain, an eternal defiance to the most complete of ours. It has that which no work emanating from the hands of man can have, the look, the smile, the warm expression—life!

The two first hours of the sitting passed like a second. I was bathed in perspiration. I took no thought of the fatigue of Mariette, whom I had only permitted to rest her arms two or three times, and I was constantly repeating: "Do not stir." Her breathing, which at regular intervals lifted her bosom with a graceful motion; the clear, white, gleaming skin, trembling with the slightest sensation of cold, touched with the flow of the fresh, warm blood coursing in her veins, all these I could have wished to hold. I was in a delirium, and no longer concentrated my mind upon my work. Through my brain passed multitudes of lines, attitudes, contours, movements, and my head was full of statues.

"Suppose you rest a little while," suggested M. Ritz, as he entered behind me.

"That is a good idea," replied Mariette; "and I will fix the fire."

She donned her skirt, threw her shawl over her shoulders, and sitting before the stove, put on some coal. I wiped my forehead and turned to M. Ritz, to ask his opinion.

"It is surprising," said he, looking alternately upon my work and myself. "It is surprising. I see I was not mistaken in you."

"Is that really true?"

"Yes. And," continued he, "I am going to take the liberty of making some remarks, although I can say to you, sincerely, that you have no longer any need of a teacher. You can go on alone, and you will succeed, because you have the love of nature in your soul; but remember this: nature is not the only end of art. Do you know what art is? It is the Beautiful within the True, and upon that principle art has created certain absolute rules which you will seek in vain to find in nature alone. If nature alone could satisfy it, you would only have to mould the form of a beautiful model, from head to foot, in order to make a chef d'œuvre. But, if you should put that idea in practice, the result would be grotesque.

"Talent consists in giving completeness to nature, gathering here and there her marvellous but partial indications, and fashioning from them a homogeneous whole, and in giving to this ensemble, a sense or a sentiment, since we cannot give it a soul. In brief, he who keeps himself within the inexorable canons of the Beautiful, comes closest to the True,—is the artist par excellence. Such was Phidias, Michael Angelo, Raphael. I have tried your merit today by a test which is decisive, and you have passed through the ordeal even more valiantly than I supposed was possible. Not the least hesitation. Full of emotion and enthusiasm. Bravo! You opened your nostrils and scented the True, as a young lion the wind of the desert. It is grand; you have succeeded, but now, this ardent impetuosity must be regulated without attenuating it.

"Stand up, Mariette; take the same pose that you had before. Very well.

"This natural position seduced you, my boy; you surprised nature in one of her artless movements, and you transfixed her ere it passed the artist's eye; but this pose, sufficient for a study, will not suffice for a statue. A woman throwing her hair behind her is all right for a six-inch statuette, to put on a mantel or a clock, but it is not worthy of high art. And then you have seen but one side of it.

"Turn around, Mariette, without changing your pose."

"See, the shoulder blades are drawn together ungracefully, the head is sunken between the shoulders, the neck is wrinkled, the back is hollowed, the loins drawn in. A statue should turn upon its base; the outlines, therefore, should be pure and bold whichever way it faces you. Now that which is presented here by nature is inexact, even deformed in some respects. What can art draw from this indication?"

Speaking again to Mariette: "Lower your arms a little, the under side is never elegant in art or nature; bring forward, and round out the angle of the elbows, hold the head straight, raise the eyes toward heaven.

"What an improvement is made by this little modification! The head slants out so that its whole contour can be seen, instead of only the chin and the nostrils being visible, when looking up to it. The hands are now held out with an agreeable gesture, where previously they were lost in the hair; while the arms, in showing the elbows on both sides, were like a pair of handles. In place of a woman merely lifting her hair, you have now, if you desire, a young martyr, chaste though naked, who is about to die, and who, in raising her hands and eyes toward the firmament, offers her life to God, and at the same time presents a beautiful form for common mortals to admire. Let us pass to the other side. The shoulder blades are now in their proper position, the neck is smooth, the back is straight, the loins are firm. Now, that the subject is adjusted, will nature suffice? In certain portions yes, in others no.

"Right here," continued M. Ritz, handling Mariette as if she were a mannikin, but with a smile expressing to her that his remarks were not personal, but applied to nature in general; "here the arms are too thin for the trunk, the hands are too large for the arms, the neck is heavy. Six heads, or six and a half at most, should be divided among seven bodies. Legs thin, ankles thick, but the remainder of the body is in marvellous proportion. You see, therefore, what to take and what to leave. Is that all? No. To what nation shall your martyr belong? Shall she be a young Greek girl who follows St. Paul to Rome? Shall she be a child of the North who went with Attila into Morvingian Gaul, and who was converted by one of the early bishops? How many different types there are. Which will you choose, and when your choice is made, where will you find the living type in these days to answer your ideal? All this is not easy," concluded M. Ritz, passing his hand across his brow, and addressing his words to himself as much as to me, "and those who go through life without seeking anything beyond, and without regard to what we are doing, are decidedly very fortunate."

Mariette dressed herself slowly, as she had undressed, concealing the beauties of her person one after another in her coarse garments, very much as a Jewish pedler puts back into his leather sack the precious stones which he has just shown you,—and she carried them all away with her, probably without having understood a word of what she had just heard.

ALEXANDRE DUMAS, FILS

III

I do not know how to explain the feeling which took possession of me when she had closed the door. I was variously impressed with what I had just seen and heard. The greatness of art and its difficulties began to be clear to me. How many illusions I must abandon. How many things I would be obliged to learn. Had I the courage?

And then there was this poor girl, who carried from studio to studio, for a little bread, the mysteries of her beauty, and who, should she die in a hospital (and where else could she die?), would serve upon the tables of a dissecting room in demonstrations of anatomy. Science would separate those limbs, in whose harmonious beauty art had sought inspiration.

This girl left me with an unconquerable feeling of sadness. For the first time, I began to think of the destiny of the mass of wretched beings who were in no way related to me. I would have liked to be useful to this Mariette, to whom I owed my first great sensation as an artist. She was no longer a stranger to me. Of that girl from whom Constantine, for instance, would have only demanded a few moments of pleasure, I retained already a grateful remembrance; perhaps it was because I found that I remained chaste through this experience. Strange trait of character! I did not want any other person to see that body, which seemed to be mine by spiritual appropriation. It was the first presentiment of the jealousy inherent in man's nature, which creates a desire in him to make his own property forever what has belonged to him for one instant. And through all these reflections I thought:

"This then is woman."

M. Ritz saw very quickly that there was something on my mind. I looked fixedly at the wall without speaking. He asked me in a hesitating way what I was thinking about. I told him without affectation.

"That is all good," he replied, "this is all good, and I congratulate myself more and more on the experiment I have made. I desired indeed to put more than a model under the eyes of an artist: I have chosen to submit a woman to the eyes of a young man, who certainly must sometimes let his thoughts run on women. I talked it over with your mother. She was very anxious about this trial. It was once for all. Which would have the mastery, the artist or the man? The artist—I did not doubt it would be so. You are well endowed, my dear boy, and I am glad to know that you are so impressed.

"There is, however, a generally accepted idea that the morals of artists are much lower than those of other classes of society, and that passion, vice, and debauchery flourish and frolic among them, as upon their native heath. It would seem quite probable, I admit, that men who are essentially occupied in things of the imagination, should gradually lose their prejudices and even their previous principles, and that the peculiar organization of these men, stretched by the tension of their faculties to a pitch which is above the ordinary diapason, should feel the need, during the interval of work, of unusual excitements, only to be satisfied by extraordinary indulgences. This is even, according to some, one of the indispensable conditions of genius. Like veritable salamanders, great artists could only live in fire, and would die in an ordinary atmosphere. By the nature of their works, artists, especially painters and sculptors, who require in order to express their ideals a direct communication with the flesh, should feel more forcibly than other men the influence of these exciting pictures.

"You have now seen for yourself, that those who believe and reason thus, are mistaken. Wherever art, that is to say the sentiment of the Beautiful, really exists, it dominates both the heart and the imagination, the senses as well as the spirit; in the moral as well as in the physical harmony of man everything must correspond. There can be no durable association between vice and genius. If these two opposite elements should by chance be combined in the same individual, one would attack and inevitably destroy the other. Examine closely the inner life of those who really deserve the name of artist, you will find them all good men, some of them as pure as saints. True genius is chaste, and its creations, whatever form they take, are chaste as itself. Immorality in the work only begins in the inferiority of the producer, who, being unable to satisfy the taste of certain judges, the leaders of public opinion, appeals to the prurient curiosity and sensuality of the crowd.

"Nevertheless these artists, however great they may be, are men withal, and if they avoid the blandishments of vice and passion, they do not escape *L'Amour*. Science may enable its adepts to forget, as it did Newton, the very existence of woman, but it is not thus with art. Imagination has its roots in the heart. If the genius of artists could be submitted to a chemical analysis, they would be found to consist, one-quarter of folly and of naiveté to three-quarters of love. Only this

ALEXANDRE DUMAS, FILS

love, after having wandered through the universe, explored space, and solicited the infinite, concentrates itself nearly always upon one single object, which seems to the lover to realize all his dream.

"I shall not tell you therefore, my boy, to love only marble, that would be useless. Everything in your organization indicates that you will love and love deeply; but ward off as long as possible that love which, next to your work, will be your life itself. Let nature develop tranquilly in you the strength which you will require to receive this inevitable guest, and, perhaps, to suffer. You will deceive yourself doubtless a few times, as many others have done, and your heart will open its door to parasites while believing it welcomes that great friend; but you will love, some time. Who? It is of little importance. To love, that is the principal thing.

"You observe that I treat you like an overgrown boy. Now, if you can make the object of your love the companion of your whole life; if the woman you love is worthy to be your wife, and if you can produce some chef-d'œuvre by the soft light of a peaceful fireside, you will have solved the problem: the grand co-existent with the Pure—the Beautiful with the Good. I desire this for you, for I love you with all my heart. I have sought this opportunity to give you, in advance, a view of life, as I discovered in you all that is necessary to comprehend it and to profit by it. In this matter, treat me as if I were your father, and anything that you cannot say to your mother, bring to me. My experience, my friendship, and my advice are at your service; as for the rest, you will excel me, which," he added with a melancholy smile, "will not be difficult."

Thus M. Ritz talked to me. I leave you to imagine how this day is graven on my memory. I have related the story at length, because it is the date of my actual entry upon my professional career. I finished the day with my mother, now entirely reassured on my account.

I returned from her house in the evening, with head uplifted and with firm tread. I felt myself a man ready to take part in all noble strife, and, I can truthfully say, with all virtuous sentiment. I wished that some one could have wanted me at once. My heart was so full. Talent, fame, and fortune were promised, and I had health, courage, and hope. In my little chamber I opened the window and looked out upon the transparent sky. I wept unseen for a full hour, and slept afterward like an infant. From that day M. Ritz and his friends began to treat me as one of their own. The most celebrated artists took an interest in me, and admitted me to their intimacy. I was soon in a position to see how true were the remarks of M. Ritz. Among the superior men of that epoch, whose reputation time has confirmed, there was not one whose private life would not bear the bright light of day.

Seek not, therefore, to defend me by any extenuation of my crime, either from the bad example which I had before my eyes, or because of the peculiar world to which I belonged. Do not, on the other hand, permit this ready-made theory to be turned against me in the hands of your adversary. I do not accept it as an argument either for or against. Vicious example has had nothing to do with the case.

There are disordered individuals, corrupt and idle, who call themselves artists because that does not commit them to anything, and in the eyes of many people is a good excuse for any kind of conduct; it is to them we owe our bad reputation. I have seen a great many of that kind of artist, dragging themselves to the studios in the morning, in the evening to the cafés to remain, perhaps, all night. They are always just about to produce masterpieces, and after having tried all their lives to outhowl each other against everything superior to themselves, they disappear, leaving no trace of their voyage of life, except the smoke of their pipes. Such persons are to artists as bankrupts are to merchants, and as deserters are to soldiers. Every class of society has its scum, and our profession is not exempt.

IV

O nce a week M. Ritz received. Having a numerous acquaintance through his special talent and by relations with artists and society people, he provided a neutral ground where they could enjoy meeting each other. Each Lundi Gras he gave a fancy dress ball, invitations to which were in great demand. At the last one of these, Mlle. Ritz met her fate in the Count de Niederfeld, a rich young Swede connected with the embassy, to whom she was married a few months after. At this same ball, Constantin, who had been at Saint Cyr for a year, wore one of those eccentric costumes which have been popularized by Gavarni. He did not remain long, and about two o'clock managed to escape, so as to finish the night at the Théâtre des Variétés, whose masked balls were the most notorious bacchanals.

The next day, by his nonchalant and blasé manner, he seemed to invite inquiry.

He told me about his first love, born at two o'clock at night, dead at eight in the morning; he remembered the costume she wore, but did not know her name.

Among the ladies I met at the ball, there was one who seemed to take a great liking to me, Madame Lespéron, a female addicted to lyric poetry, a bluestocking in fact; a silly, but very good woman.

Madame Lespéron visited at the house of M. Ritz; in return he attended her salon once a year. He swallowed the elegy, also the eau sucrée, and laughed, when at home, at that little world of ridiculous and honest people. It seems that M. Lespéron, a chief clerk in an office, one of the nicest men in the world, had begged his wife to publish her *"Douleurs"* and her *"Espérances"* under some other name than his. M. Lespéron belonged rather to the school of Désaugiers than that of Bryon. He was fond of a good table, and now and then he invited his colleagues, with their wives and daughters, and gave them a little dancing party. They dined with abundant gayety, and the poets and the muses, influenced by example, would finally join the party and consent to amuse themselves like ordinary mortals.

The same winter, which was to have so great an influence upon the destinies of so many people, Madame Lespéron also arranged at Mid-Lent a fancy dress ball, to which I was bidden. At eleven o'clock in the evening a lady entered who saluted on all sides with majestic grace. She was a woman of forty or forty-five years of age, in the dress of Marie de Médicis, as Rubens has painted it in the picture of the *Sacre*. She had ashen hair, the soft and plump flesh of a queen who feeds upon quails and sugar plums, even teeth, a round neck a trifle too short, large, white arms, and small wrists.

Her youthful beauty, judging by her present appearance, must have been remarkable, especially in the view of those epicurean philosophers, who would not that any of the good things of nature should be wasted, and who, when the summer is ended, instead of regretting it until the following spring, enjoy in October the sunshine which steals between the yellow leaves.

"These women," said an elderly intimate friend of the family, "are like *la petite Provence* of the Tuileries: one is sure to find it warm there at a certain hour."

Unfortunately for her, Marie de Médicis was followed by a page, who bore the train of her robe.

This page was a child of about fifteen years, her own daughter, azure, roses, and cream, in velvet and black satin with golden hair under her sombre cap. If the mother was a Rubens, the child was a Van Dyck. Where can I find a comparison, not to define, but to make you realize, to make you see this indefinable being?

Imagine the rose putting forth fruit of a color, shape, and flavor commensurate with the tone, form, and perfume which have always been so charming to you; seize the moment when the flower is about to change to fruit, still transparent, already firm, when the odor is intoxicating and the mouth begins to water, and you will feel, perhaps, a hundredth part of the strange sensation which this seraphic apparition produced on all the assembled guests and most of all on me.

To me, it was not a young girl, neither was it a child or a woman, it was Woman! Symbol, poem, abstraction, eternal enigma, which has caused and will cause to stumble, hesitate, vacillate, in the past, present, and future, the intelligence, the philosophies, the religions of humanity. My whole soul passed into my eyes. For the first time in my life, I could understand what had always been to me a mystery.

The historic types of women who, by breathing passion in the heart of man, have overturned empires; the feminine creations of the true poets, who filled with passion whole generations of men, and whom I had never before admired, except in their epic existence, at once became animate, and lived.

Nothing seemed to me more natural and simple than to change the whole face of the globe for the possession of one of these inexplicable beings. Eve, Pandora, Madeline, Cleopatra, Phryne, Desdemona, Manon Léscant, passed in procession before my eyes, and said to me: "Do you understand now?" And I replied: "Yes, I understand."

The queen and her page made the tour of the salon, she saluting with a little nod, he with a rosy smile. The other guests assisted at this comedy, as solemnly as the two actors, bowing to the ground like faithful subjects. I placed myself in the front rank of courtiers and devoured them with all my eyes, or rather the child, as the mother no longer interested me.

I even felt angry with her for profaning thus in public, in a costume far more indecent than the lightest and most decolleté dress, the precocious charms of her daughter. Both of them passed very near me, but without noticing me. They did not suspect that from that hour I should enter into their destiny, nothing told them with what a strange mission they were about to enter into mine. Something forewarned me doubtless, for I trembled as though shocked by electricity, when the page, with an impersonal look, thanked us collectively for our homage. I see it now.

Yes, the walls of the salon opened, I had a vision, and I saw the future face to face for a second.

The dance began again. The page was the partner of the queen. The quadrille finished, I approached the young girl and invited her for the next waltz.

"But, sir," said she with a smile, "men do not dance together."

And she turned her back to me while going to seek a young lady to dance with. She had, therefore, not only donned the costume, she was determined to play the part of a young boy. I was not vexed at that. She refused to dance with me, but, at any rate, she would only touch the hands of her own sex.

I no longer took my eyes from her. This child was the interesting feature of the soirée. The mother seated herself in a corner, where she expatiated, respirated, and fanned herself violently. Upon looking at her again, I seemed to see some unpleasant lines in that face which at first glance appeared sympathetic. The eye was cold and dry, lacking the luminous point so much sought for by painters, and which, with its beam and its dew, both illuminates and moistens the expression. The thin lips pressed closely against each other, chopping the words as they passed between them. The voice, that is to say, the soul exhaled and transmitted by sound, the most elevated and the most essential of all things to the human thinker—this voice had with her a metallic ring which dominated the general hum of conversation, very much as the sharp noise from the toolmaker's shop can be heard above the confused sounds of a village street.

Was it loss of fortune, disappointment, all the irreparable wounds of time which had so marred the features of this woman? Probably a combination of all, and ill humor had at last become one of the chief characteristics of this fat, yellow, unpleasant body. In her conversation, or rather in her monologue, for she talked on like a mechanical toy wound up to run for a certain time, the words "my daughter," "my other daughter," "her father," "my daughter's husband," were constantly repeated *à la ritournelle.*

Two or three elderly people who had resigned themselves to remain all night if necessary, until their children might be ready to leave, pretended to listen to her, and nodded their heads at regular intervals with simulated interest. In the mean while the page danced, and the line from the "Fantomes:" *Elle aimait trop le bal, c'est ce qui l'a tuée,* might have been a warning to this mother who was so proud of her daughter. After a while the child was so overcome with excitement that she retired to a deserted alcove in order to recuperate. When there, she put her hand upon her bosom, threw her head back like a little bird in swallowing a drop of water, as if she sought from above a breath of air for which she suffered.

I watched her, unseen. All of her attitudes were full of grace, each of her poses a picture. It must have been a pleasure to her to see every movement she made so faithfully repeated in the mirrors about her. However, she soon seated herself, and taking an embroidered handkerchief from her corsage, she wiped her face, unaffectedly, then she looked around at the various bric-à-brac, keeping time to the music with little nods of her head, as if her soul, unfettered, still danced on. Little by little this rhythm ceased, her lips parted, her eyes wandered, her head sank upon a cushion, her breathing became regular, her little limbs stretched out, the handkerchief dropped from her hand, her eyes closed, the child slept.

V

I was at the door of the boudoir, of which I blocked the entrance. I could have wished to keep this delicious spectacle for myself alone; the more so, because it seemed to me, at times, that I recognized the face. I had, however, never seen it before I was very sure, because it would have astonished me formerly as it was astonishing me now. But it positively resembled someone I had known.

I would willingly have remained there for the rest of the night, but Iza, (that was the young girl's name, a diminutive of Isabelle), but Iza could not leave the ball without notice being taken of it. Several young girls came to look for her; I made a signal that she was sleeping. Everybody respected this sweet sleep, which they came to admire, as for the last two hours, they had admired everything she did. The dance ceased, the orchestra was silent.

"Why don't you take a sketch?" M. Ritz suddenly said to me.

I could have embraced him before everybody for having so well divined my thought. I ran for pen, ink and paper. Ink alone could give the tones required for this beautiful dark mass. A young girl sat down to the piano and commenced to play *La Berceuse of Chopin*, which she accompanied in a soft voice. Some looked on, some listened, all were silent. The breathing of the sleeper followed the rhythm of this delicate music.

Some persons grouped behind me encouraged my hand, become as rapid as my thought, with cries of "Bravo! that's it!" Others murmured, "Hush! be quiet!" Meanwhile, the day began to dawn, and one of the company opened the curtains, while another at a sign from him blew out the lights. The ladies, surprised made their escape amidst faint screams, as if their clothing had suddenly fallen from their shoulders.

The young girl, awakened by this slight tumult, opened her eyes, looked around to see where she was, and realizing her position, smiled and sat up straight, with no regard for the presumptuous daylight, which gave to all the other countenances a ghastly pallor, but only asked from her permission to kiss her rosy cheeks. It encircled Iza like a caress, and she knew not of the triumph of her delicate beauty. Realizing that in her sleep she had been the heroine of an event of some kind, she approached me to see what I had been drawing.

"Is that for me?" she said, and put out her hand to take the sketch with childish impatience.

"Certainly, mademoiselle; but you must allow it to dry. I will frame it this morning, and if madame, your mother, consents, I will bring it to you myself."

Mother and daughter exchanged a troubled glance. "I must inform you," said the former, blushing through the rouge which in the daylight made her face seem like a mask, "that we are miserably located at present."

"Never mind, madame. But, if you prefer, I will send the drawing."

"No, bring it yourself," said the little one.

Departing, I walked behind the two ladies. In the bright street their shabby cotton-velvet costumes made my heart ache. Before stepping into the carriage which had been called for them, the mother threw about her a gray and red plaid shawl, while the daughter drew over her shoulders a black merino cloak with silk lining, much worn at the arm-holes, showing the wadding. At the direction of her mother, Iza removed her cap, handed it to her, and covered her own head with a hood of blue worsted.

Marie de Médicis put on a pair of overshoes, and turning up the train of her dress, exposed her massive legs in coarse knit stockings and well-worn satin slippers. She pushed her daughter into the carriage saying, "Get in quickly, out of the cold air." Assisted by two gentlemen, she climbed in next. Notwithstanding her royal dignity, she would have been anything but offended, if some one had hired a carriage and taken them home. I was dying to do it, but I did not dare.

Two or three gamins who stood by, shivering with cold instead of going to school, threw at the queen-mother the traditional sarcasm of the Parisian carnival.

The coachman in brown coat with triple cape, his ears protected by a dark red worsted cap, his hat askew, his large, clumsy hands in green knit gloves with red border, threatened to give them the cut with his whip. But the boys jumped out of his reach. Roguishly the little page put her head out of the window and said: "Don't forget my portrait!" Her mother called out, "Quai de l'École No. 78."

The dilapidated vehicle moved off bearing its two passengers, and, what I could not have had the least idea of, with them my life.

Returning from the ball with Constantin I could only talk of Iza, and was surprised that he did not share my enthusiasm.

"She is nothing but a baby," he remarked. "Are you going to make yourself ridiculous?"

"I can't of course have a love affair with so young a girl, but I admire her very much; she is the prettiest little creature I ever saw."

"Do you know what she reminds me of?" he asked, and his comparison was excellent. "One of Saxe's statuettes; I should be afraid of breaking it. And," he added with a laugh, "she is not high art, as my father would say. While we are on this subject, who is it she looks like?"

"I have been trying to think for more than two hours."

"It is one of our friends whom you gave a splendid blow with your fist one day."

"Minati. That's it!" I exclaimed. "Minati, that's the fellow. Why didn't I think of him before?"

"If she resembles him morally as well as physically," interposed Constantin, "she must be a very peculiar young lady. And the mother, oh, that mother! What a type. There is one who must have had adventures."

I turned the conversation. The woman and child were nothing to me, and yet I could not bear to hear anything to their disparagement. I did not go to bed, but retouched the drawing, awaiting the moment when I might present myself at the Quai de l'École. Never did time drag so. It would, however, have been very difficult for me to define the sentiment which made me so anxious to again see the charming Iza.

In love? Evidently that was not it. I could not feel that toward a little girl, whom I would probably find in a short dress, with laced shoes, a real boarding-school miss. No. This bud of a woman might have made me understand love by induction, but she could not have inspired me. Girls need be old enough to reciprocate in order to inspire, and I could never do anything half way. Either I remain absolutely indifferent to my surroundings, so that the whole world might crumble to pieces about me without causing me to turn my head, or I must throw my whole being into my sensations, however trifling they may seem to others, and entirely succumb.

Such is my nature, extreme in every way, a fact which has never permitted me to take a middle course through life. A dominating, nervous disposition that flies into a passion, and would break up any one, unless he was capable of guiding it. The events, the troubles, the reflections of my childhood, had fully developed this peculiar tendency to which I owe all the mistakes, but also all the joys and successes of life. I experienced, therefore this truly morbid agitation, which is a forerunner of fate. I was drawn to the Quai de l'École by one of those elective affinities which Goethe discovered.

Unresisting I went, and for what purpose? To see a child whose very existence was unknown to me yesterday, and who would depart in a few days, doubtless never more to cross my path, but whom I must see again, and at the earliest possible moment.

My impatience carried me beyond all bounds of propriety, and it was just mid-day when I found myself on the threshold of Iza's residence, a dingy house, which to any eyes but mine would have seemed impossible as the nest of so beautiful a bird.

VI

The house was, as it probably still is, long and narrow, with two front windows in each story, the blinds unhinged, and the small panes of greenish glass reflected the dull February sun, like tarnished tin. The loge, indicated by *Concierge* painted in large letters on the side of the stair-case, was on the left, and the visitor, feeling his way, ran great risk of striking his head against the frame of the window, behind which sat a human being, whose garments alone revealed its feminine sex, and without moving replied with a mechanical voice, according to the inquiry: "On the first," "on the second," "on the third."

"On the third," was the response to my question. I climbed the stairs, compelled to keep a strong hold on the iron rail, twisting from top to bottom like a corkscrew in a bottle. As I went up, the obscurity increased; the house was a reversed well, the light coming from below.

When I reached the landing of the third flight, I had to feel my way, and stumbled against the door. Having recovered my breath I groped for the bell-handle, and pulled it several times before it rang.

"Who is there?" queried a voice which I recognized as that of the page.

"It is I, Pierre Clemenceau," I replied. "I have brought your picture."

"Oh, I am all alone, just dressing; please wait a minute," and I heard the flic-flac of two little slippers against the floor, as they moved away. In a few minutes the door opened, and admitted me into a dark reception room. At first, I could only see the black outlines of a young girl against the inside window, with her silhouette framed in light; about the little head, a halo, like those seen in some old Byzantine picture, formed by her beautiful fluffy hair.

"Mamma has gone out," she said; "but you may step in. We did not expect you so early."

"Since your mother is already out, it would not seem much too early."

"Oh, mamma went out on business. Come into the parlor."

The room, which she dignified with the name of parlor, looked out upon the quai, the river, the bridges, the line of public buildings, which the different hours of the day colored with various tints. I realized that the dark forbidding house might be tolerated on account of this extensive horizon, sometimes grave, sometimes gay, always poetic, which cheered the sadness of those whose feet poverty has chained to earth, but whose souls have all the more need for space.

I entered the parlor, where gray paper relieved by bouquets of a lighter tint covered the walls. Upon the panel, over the piano on which were scattered sheets of music, hung a large, unframed portrait, neither very good nor very bad, of a foreign officer with heavy moustache and a profusion of decorations. A mahogany round table, a sofa in yellow damask, an easy chair in red velvet, three chairs, on the backs of which no one could lean with impunity; a work table with balls of silk, and some steel beads loose in a bonbon box, stood near the window; in front of the mantelpiece, which was ornamented with an alabaster clock and two silver-plated candlesticks, lay a rug, the pattern of which was now hieroglyphic; above the mantel a herpetic mirror, and this, with small window curtains, yellowed in the folds by sun and moisture, comprised the furniture of the room. Upon each of the chairs, I observed portions of the black costume hastily thrown off by the tired child; and in the midst of all these mean surroundings, all this dirt and disorder, stood Iza, with her youth, grace, and her unfolding life.

She was clothed in a long wrapper of blue cashmere, with swansdown boa, which she held crossed upon her bosom with her left hand. It was apparent that under this wrapper she had on only a chemise and one skirt, which from time to time peeped out in spite of her care to keep it concealed. The beautiful undulations of her form shone through the soft and yielding stuff of this bizzarre garment, which was evidently made for some one much larger than the wearer.

Iza was approaching that age when modesty begins to struggle with innocence, but where the latter, through habit, instinctively asserts itself. The curiosity to see her portrait made her at times forget the precautions indispensable to such an attire. While removing the picture from its wrapping, I saw, without seeking to do so, the budding beauty of her bosom and shoulders. With a quick movement of her foot to raise the skirt of her wrapper, she dropped one of her slippers, into which her little bare foot hopped like a bird into its nest. Tired, at last, of all these ineffectual precautions, she snatched a little scarf from a chair, tied it round her waist, and paid no further attention to her dress.

"Let me see it," she cried, approaching the window, and after a careful examination:

"How pretty it is, but how unfortunate that I was asleep, my eyes are not seen."

At this, she raised her big, blue eyes, fringed with long, brown, curling lashes.

"We will make another," I said; "two others, ten others, as many as you choose."

"When?"

"Whenever it suits you; at once, if you like."

"Not here, it is not a good place. I will come to your studio."

"Then I will also make your bust."

"Will you, really?"

"To be sure."

"But we are going away in eight days."

"That is more time than I need."

"In what will you make it?"

"In terra-cotta."

"How is that done?"

I explained the process.

"And you will send it to me?"

"Certainly."

"To Poland?"

"Yes, to Poland."

"It will be broken en route."

"I think not; or, perhaps I ought to keep it till your return?"

"I shall never return."

"What, never?"

"Never, I shall be married there."

"Ah! You are already thinking of getting married?"

"Mamma says so; I don't know. If you could only put my hands in, too, they seem to be very pretty."

And she naively showed me her hands, which were indeed marvels. Dimpled, short, tapering, with pink nails, the fingers curving backward and the joints as willing to go one way as another; and of the kind whose whiteness is not affected by the severest cold, and which are more to be distrusted than the claws of a tiger. It is perhaps upon such hands as these that nature has put the clearest indications of the tastes, of the character, and of the passions of a woman.

"How white they are," I said. "That is rarely the case at your time of life."

"I sleep in gloves. Oh! Mamma takes great care of my hands; she says that, with the feet, they are the chief beauties of a woman."

And she made a motion to show me her foot, but checked herself.

What a mixture of artlessness, of coquetry, of pride. But with what grace in all. Then, suddenly:

"We shall not be able to pay you for the bust, because we are not rich, but I will make you a handsome purse. See, what pretty ones I can make." Then she showed me little bits of her work, which were what they should be from such hands as hers, and I was busy looking them over, somewhat abstractedly, when the door opened noisily. A husband wishing to surprise his wife would have opened it in the same manner. It was the mother. I rose with a start; Iza merely turned her head.

"It is mamma. How did you come in?"

"The janitor told me there was a young man here."

"Well, here he is."

"But it is not right for him to be here."

"Why not?"

"Because it is not proper; and I don't see why the gentleman came at such an hour to call upon respectable ladies, with whom he is unacquainted, and why he should remain with a young girl in the absence of her mother."

I mumbled an excuse.

Iza interrupted me, and made some remarks in Polish to her mother.

The countess changed her manner at once, and took the portrait, saying to her daughter: "Go and dress yourself, darling."

"You understand of course," she answered, placing the portrait on the table without looking at it, "that a maiden is very easily compromised, it takes but a minute to do it, and in our position the least bit of slander would do us great harm. As to Iza, I mean; but for myself, I am no longer subject to it. If I had not watched closely over my other daughter, she would not have made the marriage she did, and of which she was worthy, for she belonged to one of the oldest and most noble Polish families; but we were not rich, and in all countries, Poland as well as France, wealth is the great thing."

"My husband was ruined by the last insurrection. He believed in independence, and he was foolish. The Emperor of Russia made him some splendid propositions, which he refused. His brother accepted them and did well. He occupies now one of the highest places at St. Petersburg. He was the younger brother, but, since the death of Jean (my husband's Christian name) he is the sole representative of the family. Our property was confiscated. I have not the same reasons that

Jean had, to be a patriot (I am not Polish myself, but Finnish), I applied to my brother-in-law to intercede with the Emperor in our favor. I have recently received some good news, and that is why we are going away.

"My eldest daughter is married to a very rich man, but she had no dowry, and you know how it is with children when once they are fixed themselves; she does not trouble herself about me. She writes me letters when she feels like it, but there is nothing in them but words. I cannot really count upon her. She is pretty, but not nearly so pretty as Iza. What a success she had last evening. It is the same where-ever we go. That girl will some day sit on a throne, I know what I am talking about. She has the instincts of a queen, and I have my own ideas on the subject.

"In Russia, marriages of poor girls with princes are not unfrequent. Peter the Great married a servant, and he was himself the son of a woman born far from the throne, and chosen by his father among the nobility of the kingdom. My daughter is noble, as much so as the Radzywill and the Czartonyski. When younger, she often played with one of the Emperor's sons during his visits to Warsaw. They were only children, but he has not forgotten her; I have it from reliable authority, and when he sees her again his affection will revive. He is not the hereditary prince, it is true, but he has a chance with the others; no one can say who will live or who will die in the Russian Imperial families, and, while waiting, they will be less particular about a younger scion, and will doubtless permit him to marry as his heart may dictate.

"I am bringing up Iza with that view; she speaks four languages, French, English, Polish, and Russian. Apropos, you must make a handsome portrait of her. This sketch is very well, but I need something more; one that I can have brought under the eyes of the prince. I have there still another friend besides my son-in-law, who would be the first to oppose my projects if he knew them, through jealousy; instead of seeing that his own interest would be served by such an alliance, for Iza would not forget her own relations. She is very good, that little darling; she has a heart, she works like a little fairy, and accepts cheerfully all privations.

"There is nothing about it to be ashamed of, but I can tell you, young man, you who have to work for your living, we have seen some days since we have been in Paris, when we have not had a single sou. However, Iza sang, and we have often lived by the work of our hands. A Dobronowska, selling purses made by herself! Perhaps you will ask me then why we went to the ball; it is necessary to have a little change, the poor little dear, and I understand that this Madame Lespéron is acquainted with some influential people. Perhaps they might be useful to us.

"She recently introduced us to the manager of a theatre, who offered me a salary of four thousand francs a year if I would let him have my daughter. Iza has a lovely voice. He promised to pay me that salary until she should make her first appearance, and not to bring her out until she had received the necessary training. He would take entire charge, and pay all expenses, regardless of the number of masters required. I refused, indeed I did, for a girl like that. However, I could not blame the gentleman, who knew nothing about us whatever. I only mention it to give you an idea of the impression that Iza produces at first sight. Nevertheless I would much prefer to see her on the stage with talent, and earning two hundred thousand francs a year, than have her married to a bourgeois, who could not understand her.

"Just think of that girl as the wife of a tradesman. She is born to shine, it makes no difference where, but on the summit; it is essential, however, that she should not be talked about beforehand; therefore, I watch over her carefully. She is innocence itself, and I know very well that she has never seen nor heard the faintest thing which can set her thinking.

"As to myself, I have never had the least little bit of an adventure, although I have been very beautiful, and even now, if I was so inclined, I could be married again, and well too, but I don't care. And this is why, when I learned Iza was in company with a young man—I did not know, of course, that it was you; or, if I had known, I should still have hurried up-stairs, because, after all, I am not acquainted with you, and young men, you know, are always ready to take whatever they can find.

"Every day, when in the street, somebody follows us, because we have not the means to take a carriage. Iza seems older than she is—fifteen years lacking two months—just think of it, she is a little woman, ravishingly formed; such a model would make the fortune of an artist; but you can't find anything like that among the lower classes, from which you are obliged to obtain your recruits. Formerly, great ladies posed nude, before painters and sculptors. Today, they would not hear of such a thing. What times! Besides, some of the beauties are aristocratic. Her father was splendid, he was one of the handsomest men you ever saw. That is his portrait, I always carry it with me, notwithstanding the trouble, for it is very large. I have sold the frame, which I could not take about, but then I have been compelled to do a good many things.

"Where do you suppose I came from just now? Ah. Mon Dieu! I will tell you. I came from the pawnshop. That explains why I went out so early, I have been to pledge a jewel which the Austrian Ambassador gave Iza in return for a present of some of her fancy work to his daughter. But for that gem I don't know what would have become of us. What I have told you is entirely confidential; I would die of shame if any one knew of our position. Besides, we are expecting some money from Poland; but while waiting, we must live."

"O madame," I said with emotion as soon as I could put in a word; "I am not rich, and I understand better than most what it is to be poor, but I can earn some money, and if I were permitted to render you a service, I assure you it would be a great pleasure to me."

"You are a nice child," said the countess, taking my hands, "but just now we do not require anything. When we take our departure, should we need something, I promise you, I will let you know. Fortunately, we have no rent to pay; this apartment is loaned to us by an old gentleman whom I have known in other days, and who permits us to occupy it while he is travelling; he is in ill health, and spends the winter with his son in the south. It is not handsome, but it has been a great economy for us."

Iza returned, all muffled up in winter clothes.

They were going out, and it was the mother's turn to dress. I again remained alone with the child, whose mobile features had suddenly taken on an expression of sadness, almost of suffering. Her big eyes were wider open than before, her cheeks were pale and her lips had lost some of their color. She seated herself in front of the window, and looked out at the dull day, evidently making an effort not to appear ill.

"What makes you look at me that way?" she queried

"You appear to be suffering," I said, "and I am anxious about you."

"My head is a little dizzy; that often happens when I have not slept enough."

"Why did you go to the ball?" I asked. "It is the fatigue of that."

"Mamma wished me to go; and besides it was quite necessary."

"Necessary? Why so?"

"Oh, because it was."

She made no other reply.

"But that is not all," I went on; "you remind me so much of one of my old companions."

"A boy?"

"Yes, he was a boy."

"I thank you for the compliment."

"But a boy handsome as a girl."

"What was his name?"

"André Minati."

"Indeed, when did you know him?"

"In M. Fremin's boarding school, where he died."

Iza called: "Mamma!"

"What is it?" asked the countess from the other room. Her daughter made a long remark in Polish, watching me from the corner of her eye to be sure that I did not comprehend. The mother responded by a monosyllable which appeared to be in the negative. "Well," said Iza, returning to our conversation, as if she had only interrupted it in order to convey to her mother some thought, which had no reference to us. "Well, I am much pleased to have reminded you of a friend. You will remember me longer on that account."

The Countess entered.

"Now come," she said; "we must be going. It will do you good to get out." Then, turning to me:

"Have you seen her hands?"

"I have," I replied.

"Look at them," and she raised her daughter's hands that I might admire their truly remarkable transparency, as she held them between my eyes and the light. Folding the hands in her own, she kissed them with a sort of frenzy, saying:

"You are a beauty, there's no doubt about it."

That remark had the effect of a cordial on the child, and her cheeks flushed, she smiled, and recovered her strength. We went down to the street together.

I accompanied the ladies to the Champs Élysées.

Among all the promenaders whom we met, fashionable or otherwise, none were too much preoccupied to render homage to the fair young face at my side. Nearly every one turned for a second glance. Occasionally some one would stop straight in our path and stare, compelling us to bend our course to the right or left, in order to continue on our way.

Iza did not seem to perceive the flutter she caused, and it was evident that she could have walked all day without fatigue.

It was arranged that she should come to pose for me on the following day, and I bade adieu at Place Louis XV, surmising they would prefer to continue alone. Yet, I could not resist the temptation to follow in the wake of admiration.

Being Sunday, there was a great crowd, and as they walked leisurely up the Grand Avenue of the Champs Élysées, the same impression was produced the whole length of the route. They went as far as la barrière de l'Etoile, then down to the Faubourg du Roule, came to la rue Verte and disappeared in a large house, where they dined. As I had followed them only through curiosity, I returned to my home, or rather my mother's, and naturally related all that had happened since the previous evening. Iza was but fifteen. In eight days she would be gone; my mother, no more than myself, suspected danger. I also told her of all my surprises, for I could not exactly understand everything that I had seen and heard.

The apparition of the page, the dilapidated lodging, the poverty, the coquetry, such innocence, such ambition, the throne, the pawn shop, all this confused me as much as the child interested me. In fact, I could have understood any one of these things with its direct consequences. I could have comprehended the poverty, the pawnbroker, the toil, the sorrow, and the present resignation; the hopes for the future, however vague. But the disparity between the penury and their appearance at the ball; the apartment of the old gentleman and the alliance with the Czar; the purses for a livelihood and the gloves for sleeping in, I could not take in, as is vulgarly said, never having met with a world where these contrasts are in vogue.

My mother failed to fathom it either, and merely said:

"This lady has neither order nor common sense, which is unfortunate for her daughter, since you say that she is pretty and apparently good."

M. Ritz, to whom I likewise narrated the story of my visit, and the impression it had left upon me, contented himself with saying:

"Life only can explain the strange thereof. Make a handsome bust of this girl, make even a full length statue of her, if her mother proposes it to you, as it is possible she will, and don't worry about the rest. She is neither your sister nor your daughter."

The next day the mother and her child came to the studio at the appointed hour. I commenced the bust, the features of which I have given to my figure of the *Premier Réveil*, that became the foundation of my reputation. In three days it was finished; then I moulded the hands of this charming model, then her feet. Babouchka (a familiar, too familiar, name which Iza gave to the countess, and which signifies old grandmother) had so great admiration for the beauty and for the beauties of her daughter, that I believe she would have unveiled them all, as M. Ritz suggested she would, if I had insisted, so delighted was she to meet an admiration as fervent as her own.

The sojourn of the two ladies at Paris was prolonged, and we formed the habit of seeing each other every day.

When at my studio, Iza made herself entirely at home. We remained together there, four or five hours at a time, which she spent in laughing, playing, embroidering, singing, or sleeping, for she followed her impulses in everything, and soon became part of my work, of my thought, of my life. The incessant talk of her mother was no longer disagreeable to me. I even began to enjoy it, as with those oriental melodies, which at first jar upon you with their discordant notes, but little by little wrap you in their monotonous rhythm, and soothe you, permitting only a vague and undefined idea of the harsh harmony to enter your consciousness.

I no longer sought to explain the sentiment with which this beauteous girl inspired me; I abandoned myself to it like a child, like an artist. I found a joy in being near her, as we enjoy the sun in the early days of April. Her presence gave me that fulness of faculty of which we seldom find ourselves possessed, when the whole body and soul correspond in a perfect equilibrium. My heart and my brain positively enlarged under this new influence. When left alone, I rushed out and walked for hours. Then we would take long rambles together and finally enter a restaurant. Ordering dinner and generously pouring out wine, as with a comrade, I would talk to her of the future, of Art, of the Beautiful; and then escorting her home, kiss her repeatedly, and retiring, instantly fall asleep.

At eleven o'clock in the morning, Babouchka and her daughter came, and we commenced the delightful day where we had left off the previous evening. On two or three occasions, the mother related some anecdotes of her country, in a good-natured vein. She was witty when she forgot herself, and made Iza and me laugh heartily, as was natural to our growth. I could have lived in this way ten thousand years. One day I involuntarily cried out before them:

"I would gladly pass my whole life in this way."

"And I too," replied Iza.

"Mamma, why can't we remain at Paris?"

"You know very well that is impossible," she rejoined. "What would you do with yourself here?"

"Grow up, and marry M. Clemenceau; isn't that what you'd like to have me do?"

"Most certainly," said I.

"A pretty arrangement," exclaimed the mother. "Why, neither of you have any money."

"So very little is necessary," I ventured. "And I will earn money to keep all comfortably."

"Listen," said Iza, "if I don't find the king or the prince that mamma promised me, I promise you, myself, that I will marry you. Is it agreed?"

"It's a bargain."

"Wouldn't it be funny if it should happen?" and she laughed heartily.

"In the mean while," continued the mother, "we depart tomorrow, and it is quite probable that we shall not return."

At the close of the scene, the countess took me aside and said:

"My dear young friend, I feel toward you as if you were one of my own family, and although I could ask of others the favor I am about to request of you, I prefer to be under obligations to you, especially since your offer to assist me, and in fact, I should hesitate to expose my situation to any one whom I did not love. My daughter needs many little things for the journey; we are short of money. Could you lend me five hundred francs, which I will send to you from Warsaw as soon as we arrive? There is a considerable sum of money awaiting me there. But do not let Iza know anything of this."

I could have kissed "Babouchka" for the pleasure she afforded me. Something of mine was to go with these two ladies, to whom I owed so much delight during the past month; for at the moment of separation, my heart, blending the old and the young, made of the grotesque and the graceful but one image.

I told her I would make a farewell call that evening and bring the amount mentioned. We met by appointment at a restaurant near Palais Royal at six o'clock, and I slipped the five-hundred-franc note into Babouchka's hand. At the table I selected the choicest dishes on the menu with the lavish inexperience of a poor young man. The countess drank freely and was more voluble than ever. In her semi-intoxication anybody but myself would have noticed many things at variance with remarks previously made by her, but I had no thought for anything beyond the pleasure of remaining with these two friends, whom upon the morrow I might lose forever. Iza was wildly gay. At dessert she sang like a bird, with interludes of happy prattle: "When I am rich, I will have this, I will do that," as if there was not the slightest doubt she would be rich, very rich, some day.

I went home with them, and bade them adieu. I promised to forward the bust, the sketches, and the medallion, which were not yet completed. We agreed to correspond, and to keep each other informed as to our welfare. The countess assured me she would see that I received some orders from the Emperor of Russia, and embraced me when we separated. Iza, in her turn, held her face up for me to kiss, in the most artless manner, and without waiting to be asked.

"Au revoir, my little husband," she said.

"Au revoir, my little wife," I replied, and, pressing my hand as if we were actually engaged, she disappeared in the hallway of Quai de l'Ecole.

As a matter of fact, both Iza and myself had our hearts in our eyes.

Would you believe it, my friend, I took those words: "My little husband, my little wife," seriously, and said to myself, "why not?" They became the goal of my work and my fortunes. I loved, there was no doubt about it, with all the adoration one could have for a child, but my soul trembled under this first ray of love, as the earth under the first rays of morning, the dawn which heralds sunrise. The engagement strengthened me in my secret resolutions. Even if it came to naught, I should have had my Beatrice, who would protect me from vicious attachments. This was my resolve; I can admit it now, when I no longer fear ridicule.

Besides, I had a long time ago made a solemn vow to marry only for love, and to bring her a virgin heart and body. In the first place, I could not cause any woman, whoever she might be, the misery a man had brought on my mother; troubled my life and embarrassed my career. How many artists have I known, full of promise, whose bright prospects were suddenly blighted by some illicit love, which, though apparently of no consequence, dragged in its train disorder, poverty, and mental sterility. This little romance, therefore, harmonized with my programme, and I returned to my work with the idea that it was to establish a reputation, and to acquire a competence within two or three years, that I might marry the girl of my choice. Was not this a romantic dream for a twenty-year-old young man?

However, my chastity, which this incident confirmed, was for my fellow-artists, less sentimental than myself, a perpetual subject of surprise and ridicule. They soon went so far as to account for my continence, the motive for which I had never revealed to any one, in some other way than as the result of my own will. I was compared to Narcissus, Joseph, and to that son of Mercury and Venus, whom the nymph Samalcis was unable to seduce. They sent me the most beautiful, the most tempting, and the most willing creatures. I admired them, I modelled from them, and when their advances became too pronounced, I merely said, that I had no time to waste.

I had besides, among both ancients and moderns, examples to sustain me. For instance, every one knows that our great painter S——, imitator of Raphael, while safe in this veneration of nature, went to such an extent as to kneel before the beautiful girl who served him as a model. He kissed with the tips of his lips that portion of her form which seemed to him the most perfect, treated her as he would a goddess, and thanked God for having created her. He called this adoration the Mass of art. I belonged to his school, except the kiss.

I chose my subjects instinctively from modest legends. I was always imbued with admiration for the nude; I believe it art *par excellence*, the noblest and grandest, but, at the same time, the most dangerous. If it were only revealed to men of refinement, or to men of matured character, there would be no objection to it; exposed, however, to all passers by, it becomes an object for the gratification of precocious curiosity, a source of information that is too precise, alluring young imaginations.

I was more than ever full of these ideas, after the departure of Iza. I carved my statue of Claudia, the suspected vestal, who had only to attach her girdle to the ship which bore the statue of Cybele to bring it into the Tiber, despite contrary winds. Traditional power of virginity! Jeanne d'Arc repeated this miracle before Orleans, only this Christian virgin had no need to remove her girdle. By prayer alone she caused the boats to sail up the Loire against wind and stream.

My Claudia was a brilliant success, and several of my friends decided to celebrate the event by giving me a dinner.

A plot which I did not suspect was hidden beneath this compliment.

Only men were invited, and it was to take place in the elegant studio of Eugene F——. I accepted the invitation with more pleasure than pride in my success at this opening of my career. The presence of M. Ritz prevented any distrust on my part. He was incapable of countenancing any improprieties. But M. Ritz, as was his habit, retired long before the banquet was finished, and the others made me drunk. It was not difficult, since I usually drank nothing but water.

You are of course aware to what extremes freedom supervenes after a hearty dinner, among a company of young and independent artists. They laughingly mentioned certain insinuations laid at my door, and gave me advice how to act under various circumstances.

Well, do you know my reply to these jests, to these epigrams, to these strange provocations? All at once, in a fit of drunken bravado, I arose,—I threw gold upon the table, and, amid the plaudits of all the convives, I, the chaste, the modest, the pure Clemenceau, made the grossest and most unheard-of wager. I felt the brutal, blind, and monstrous passions of rape and murder rush to my brain, and almost suffocate me. What manner of man was this whom liquor had suddenly aroused? Was I so little master of my own will, that a few glasses of red or white wine had the power to transform me into a wild beast, a boon companion for a time of the notoriously dissolute?

It is said, God has invested mankind with freedom of choice. Who says so? Those who believe it; for God has confided to no one, neither his intentions, nor the elements of which his creatures are made. If he has given this freedom of choice, he only dispensed it to the first man who went forth from his hands without the assistance of any human being, and we know, according to tradition, to what use that man put his endowment when under the spell of a woman, who was formed from him. With Cain, the freedom of choice disappeared. Cain is no longer master of his deeds. He is the son of his father. The father was culpable, the son criminal, the transmission has begun, the hereditary law asserts itself, and it is never recalled. Like father, like son.

Doctors will tell you that they have often observed in their patients a strange disease come suddenly upon them; chronic, rather than acute; constitutional, but with no precursory symptoms; organic, but unlike anything else in the system, and not in accord with their temperament or their habits. Upon interrogating the invalid or his parents, they find, in going back one, two, three, or more generations, the origin and cause of this sudden manifestation.

It is the same with moral maladies. They are inherited; insanity proves this. Ever since the second man, we are no longer the creatures of God; every one of us is the product of two organizations, which love, pleasure, interest, or chance have brought together, and we carry within ourselves, equal or unequal portions of the double individuality which we have received. If the two progenitors were sympathetic, congenial, parallel so to speak, the product has every chance of being in harmony with himself; equable, adequate, as the doctors say; if there is a difference in the natures, an antagonism between the paternal and the maternal types, the child will inevitably come under these contrary influences, until one shall triumph over the other.

So it seems that, until this episode, I had been dominated by the gentle maternal influence, with the exception of a day when I rushed upon my schoolmate André Minati, and nearly strangled him. In the incongruous, monstrous act which I committed on the night of the banquet, the father principle had again obtruded itself, and overruled my theories and habits more brutally than before. That father, whom I had never known, and yet held latent within me, announced himself, and, quick as lightning, asserted the occult law of transmission the very instant the environment was favorable. The more fatal, since I knew nothing about him; therefore at a loss how to oppose him. Thus far he had only revealed himself in violence, and, when I felt a bad impulse, I said to myself: "Here is the Unknown."

Alas! I was not always on the alert to unmask him, and, at last, I was conquered in the struggle.

At home, after the bet had been won, my memory and better self returned, and I kneeled before my image of Iza imploring forgiveness, swearing to love only her. The shame of my reprehensible conduct overwhelmed me. I made Iza my patron saint, my guardian angel, my protecting virgin; I promised to render her an account of my daily life, and do nothing that should cause her to blush.

Vice, upon those to whom vice is not the normal condition, and who are capable of repentance, produces a curious effect. It seems to change the absolute plans of goodness, and gives the appearance of positive honesty to those who are only relatively so. Thus Iza and her mother were, logically, two adventuresses, one of whom had finished and the other about to commence her career, though I was blind to the fact. Compared to the vile and degraded creatures with whom I had spent the night, they seemed like saints. I saw them in the light of my imagination; I only remembered the mother's good nature, the grace, the innocence, the beauty of the daughter, and those days of work and intimacy which were in such flagrant contrast with the spectacle of the previous evening. Henceforth, Iza was to me a portion of the celestial host.

However, despite my resolutions, my contempt for that first woman, and the unpleasant recollections of the whole scene, that first woman did not go out of my life as quickly as I hoped. The new sensation to which she had introduced me, left the same effect as a sound drawn sharply from a stringed instrument produces on the air. For a long time I felt the vibration of that acute note.

That creature was a beautiful brunette, with luxuriant hair, black as ink, and with metallic lustre, a low forehead and heavy eyebrows. Her eyes shone beneath their long lashes like emerald and silvery fishes which gleam through water grasses on the river's bank.

My friends were ashamed of their sportiveness when they saw what came of it, and apologized with as much gravity as possible under the circumstances. One of them told me that Claudia (for the name of the vestal had been given to that girl) was passionately fond of me. A real triumph, for she had no more heart than the beautiful Imperia, the automaton of the Contes d'Hoffman.

I don't know what impression I had made upon the courtesan, but I met her two or three times afterward, and each time I trembled, and I saw that she turned pale. There was between us a bond, unacknowledged, but real. The senses have their memories.

I applied myself to work more desperately than ever, and with no other distraction than Iza's letters.

I have preserved all the correspondence, and I will give it to you entire.

My Dear Friend
"Do not blame me for not writing you before this. At first we were much fatigued, because it was a long route, and, at this season of the year, a bad one. Notwithstanding our anxiety to arrive promptly and to travel with economy, we were obliged to rest one night at Cologne, and another at Breslau, and the hotels there are very expensive. We reached Warsaw a long time ago. I am an ingrate, I hear you say. Every day I have wanted to write, but mamma has been sick, and we have had much to do.

"O my good friend, how I regret Paris and those pleasant days in your studio! I have often thought of you. Do not forget that you are my little husband. I am not jesting. I will return, and we will be married. Mamma forbids me to speak of that, because, she says, it is not proper, but I can't help telling you that I love you with my whole heart, and that I wish I was at your side, or you were at mine.

"Have you finished my bust? When will you send it? I believe that it would be better to omit the flowers in the hair.

"Mamma says my hair is so long and so beautiful, that it does not need any ornament. The truth is they dressed it *à la grecque*, which is very becoming to me, for the soirée at the Lord Chamberlain's, where I made quite a sensation. I had a very good time, but it was not as lively as at Madame Lespéron's. Au revoir, my dear friend. Write often and don't forget me. Mamma sends you many kind regards. She will write you very soon. For myself, I present my most sincere respects.

Your little wife,
Iza Dobronowska

"P. S.—As soon as the bust is finished, please send it to the embassy, in care of the secretary. He is one of our friends. In that way it goes free."

Four months after:

"You must have been surprised, my dear friend, not having heard from us for so long a time, and that we have not thanked you for the bust. A well-known art amateur here has pronounced it very beautiful. He told mamma, if she would sell it he would give two thousand francs for it. Mamma declined of course.

"Only yesterday we returned to Warsaw, after a business trip to St. Petersburg. Mamma hoped to have an audience with the Emperor, but he was absent at Odessa.

"We saw my sister at St. Petersburgh. How pretty she is. My brother-in-law, who is aide-de-camp of the Emperor, went with him. My sister obtained for us an audience with the grand duke. He was very well dressed, but he did not seem to take notice of me. My mother says he is a very grave man, and does not care for women. I don't understand very well what that means, but I think it is very nice to see a pretty woman. The grand duke told mamma he would look into our affairs. My sister gave me some dresses, and a handsome bracelet.

"Write us often, and tell us what is going on in Paris. We find it very tedious sometimes. Au revoir, dear husband.

Your little wife, who kisses you

Iza

August 18—

"How kind it was of you to remember my birthday and to send a flower in your letter. I have received several presents, but none so pleasing as your souvenir. Mamma is more cheerful, our affairs being in better shape.

"She has found an officer, the son of a distant relative of ours, who is very influential with the grand duke. He is very clever and has beautiful horses. He promised to recover all our property, and mamma says he spoke to her about me as if he wanted to marry me; but she says he is not rich enough. His income, I understand, is at least two hundred thousand francs a year. That is pretty good, but my poor mamma is always dreaming of a throne. He has given me a ring. It's a very beautiful turquoise, the bluest of blue, with a diamond on each side. It is worth five hundred francs and suits me exactly. Mamma sends her compliments. Adieu, my dear friend.

Iza

November 18—

"I have let a long time pass without writing you, because mamma has been sick, and our affairs have gone from bad to worse. Fortunately, during her convalescence, we stopped in the country at the house of an aunt of that young man I wrote about in my last letter. She had gone away for a whole year, and gave us the privilege of her chateau, which is very large and very handsome, with trees more than a century old. It is quite lonesome out in the country. We have seen nobody except this young man, who has been several times to visit us, just as if it were not his own home. He has taught me to ride horseback. This exercise has done me much good. I was coughing a little, I do not cough now, and I have grown at least two inches. If our affairs do not improve, we shall spend the winter here notwithstanding the cold; but there are large stoves in all the halls, the same as in town, and, then it is so necessary for us to economize. Au revoir, my dear friend, do not forget

Your Iza

Dear Sir

"I have to apologize to you for not having yet returned the little sum which you so kindly loaned me. Iza has doubtless told you that we have had much annoyance in the matter of our claim. She does not know, poor little thing, how much trouble I am taking that she may some day be rich and happy like her sister, who could easily show more gratitude than she does. We have never been so miserable as since our return, but I am not ashamed. There are names that misfortune makes all the more illustrious, and this was never more true than in our case. At last the sky begins to brighten, and I believe that in a little, very little while, we shall see the end of our trouble.

"In the mean while, I enclose, with a thousand thanks, my dear sir, the five hundred francs you loaned me, which have been very useful to us. Remember me, I beg, to your excellent mother, and believe me, with affection and gratitude,

Countess Dobronowska

No other letter for a year, then:

My Dear Friend

"Will you do me a favor? Ask your mother how much she would charge for a complete trousseau, everything of the finest linen, and in the most elegant style, with monograms and coronets; there will also be a gentleman's night gown and robe de chambre. It is the custom here for the bride to provide these two articles. The bill will be paid cash on receipt of same, or half in advance if necessary. Answer immediately.

Your old friend,
IZA DOBRONOWSKA

"I did not expect, monsieur, to receive such a letter, almost impertinent, which you have written me. It was only a slight favor that I asked, as your mother was a seamstress when we left Paris two years ago. I was not aware that she was not one still; it was therefore quite natural that I should apply to you. It is not dishonorable to work for a living, my mother and myself have often worked for ours. I am none the less pleased, however, to learn that your mother is no longer under that necessity, and, I remain, monsieur,

Yours with respect,
IZA DOBRONOWSKA

Another year without a word, and then:

"I am in great trouble. Why is it that you are the first person to whom I feel like telling it? Do you think of me sometimes? Do you detest me? I do not ask if you are still alive, because you are so famous, that I should have heard if you were dead; but tell me, are you happy, as I hope you are? And if there is at the bottom of your heart, a bit of kind feeling for your naughty and unhappy little Iza, who has great need of the advice and friendship of her dear friend. Do not direct to me any more Place du Palais, we have moved. Address your letter Rue Piwna, in care of Mademoiselle Vanda. I don't want mamma to know that I have written to you. My poor mamma is in very bad health, and is very sad.

I

"How good you are, and how I love you, my dearest friend. I was right in not doubting your kindness. I cried over your letter. You ask me what has happened. Mamma's hopes have not been realized, neither for herself nor for me, and we have never before been in so sad a plight as at present. You know mamma. She is easily deceived, and she is always so confident.

There was a prospect of a marriage for me, which, though neither royal nor princely, was better than anything I had dreamed of. I sacrificed myself for her. The young man was distinguished and rich, but I did not love him. He proposed, and it was agreed upon. I don't know what influenced his family, but he was compelled to break the engagement. In the mean time we had spent money foolishly, which was to be paid upon my marriage. Indeed Serge, for that was his name, encouraged us in this, and mamma thought to hold him more firmly by that means, since he was cognizant of our pecuniary situation, and thus became morally responsible for these expenditures. When his friends learned of his intentions, they violently opposed it; and as he was a minor, and could not marry without the consent of his parents, who threatened to disinherit him, he wanted to take me to England and marry me there. But what would have become of us without finances? His father, who is very influential, proposed to have us imprisoned, both mother and me. We were helpless, so mamma yielded on condition that she should be repaid all the money we had spent, but we lost a good deal notwithstanding, because poor mamma had no system, and she forgot a good many things. They sent Serge abroad. He writes me that he still loves me, and that I must wait for him, and that he will marry me as soon as he is of age, but I do not answer his letters. The affair made a great deal of talk, and mamma nearly died from the effects of it, and one result of it is, that we are not on good terms with my sister and her husband, who are glad to have an opportunity to get rid of us. Our means are diminishing. We sell, little by little, the jewelry that Serge gave me, and which he did not wish me to return. Without that I don't see how we should live. Advise me, my dear friend. Ah, how fortunate you are to be a man, and to have talent, and to live in a free country! In France, they could not have treated me as they have treated me here. Fortunately, I have a fine voice, and I am growing prettier all the time; I can give singing lessons. It is hard, but we must live. I was offered an engagement at the theatre of St. Petersburg with a salary of five thousand silver roubles, which is nearly twenty thousand francs, but mamma is strongly opposed to my going on the stage. She does not give up the idea of marrying me, either to Serge or to somebody else; but I don't want any more such experiences. Advise me. I will do whatever you say. Serge is at Vienna; he writes me that he is going to Paris. When he does, he will surely see you. I have talked to him about you often, so often that he did not want me to write to you any more. He was jealous, and with reason. I loved you, and I love you more than I do him. I hope you are in Paris, and that my letter will reach you. I shall watch for an answer with great impatience."

"Au revoir, my dear friend, and do not forget your little friend of long ago,

Iza

"Why should I reproach myself? I did nothing to make Serge fall in love with me. He came of his own accord. Besides, mamma never left us alone together. He called himself, in her presence, my little husband, just as you did yourself. Only you were not in earnest while he was, because I was two years older than when in Paris, and I dressed still older, and it is natural that people should fall in love with me; however, I did not think of that at the time. Mamma permitted me to go on without saying anything, and it was only when he asked for my hand, that she spoke to me about it. What would you have had me do? I have no fortune, not even anything to live on. If my mother should die, what would become of me? I have no right to think of myself only, I must think of her who has brought me up, and who has based on me all her hopes of wealth and happiness, and with her, one of these is impossible without the other.

"Do you think the life I have led for several years is according to my tastes? To be always exhibited in public, like a curious animal, to hear how beautiful I am without anything coming of it? I don't think that very amusing. It was my mother's idea. Many times we have gone hungry to a ball, after having pawned our most necessary articles to buy me a dress. Oh, the debts, the worry, the scenes with creditors upon whom the beauty, which was to bring me millions, had not the slightest effect. Serge was to have an immense fortune. In marrying him, all our troubles would cease. I did not really love him, but he was a good fellow, and I had a warm friendship for him. My mother said it would be a magnificent marriage. I am not ambitious on my own account. If I could consult my own inclinations, I would like to marry a man whom I loved, and to spend all my time with him. Beauty is not all. There are plenty of girls as beautiful, more beautiful than I am, and rich at the same time, and they are the kind that rich men marry. You should not reproach me, when I ask for your advice.

"While waiting for your reply, I consented to sing at a concert given by my singing teacher. I was greatly applauded. He promised to divide the receipts with me; he only gave me five hundred francs; that is always the way. If I was sure of getting as much every time I sang, I would sing every day; it does not fatigue me in the least.

"How unfortunate that you do not understand me, and would not tell me sincerely your opinion. You are not willing that I should go on the stage. You say it is too dangerous for me. What is the danger? Well, then, find me a husband, some man who wants a good little wife, and who is not particular about the dowry. That is the essential point. Tell him that I will love him truly, and that I will sing only for him, but you must find him quickly, for the winter is coming, and the aunts are not lenders in Poland any more than in France. If you were really kind, you would send me your picture. You also must be changed. I will send you mine. I did not have it made for you, but I am quite sure I have no better friend, so I will give it to you. Adieu, monsieur, I don't love you any more; you are too disagreeable, and too ready to believe bad things of

Iza Dobronowska

"I do not even wait your reply, my very dear friend, to call to you with all my strength: Save me, I beg of you, and do not let me remain as I am! I would tell you all, if you were here, but I cannot write it, it is too dreadful, and a child should not accuse her mother whatever she may do, but for heaven's sake, come to my rescue. It is absolutely necessary that I should return as quickly as possible to France, and I want to come alone. To remain with my mother is impossible. If you knew what a scene we have had, and the cause of it. Do not ask me to write it. Think how you would feel, if you were obliged to say anything against your mother; but then you are a man. By all that is sacred to you, seek and find some way for me. Could I not live with your mother? I would give singing lessons, teach; I speak English better than I do French, in which I am not very perfect, but I will learn. I only ask some means of earning my living. They may say of me what they choose, that I am a bad girl, that I have run away with a lover; no matter, I shall have my own clear conscience, and your esteem. If I had the money, I would start this very evening. I am almost wild. One of my friends would lend me her passport, but that is all she can lend me. I ask you only this, if you can't assist me in this matter, never mention this letter to my mother nor to yours, who would think ill of me, supposing that all mothers are like herself. I have thought of entering a convent, but I am afraid I would not have the courage to remain there. I feel that I have the strength and the will to be a good woman, but in the world, among people. If your mother will not take me, perhaps M. Ritz's daughter would? She has a child of three years, she might take me for a governess? Or that Madame Lespéron, at whose house I first saw you (oh, that happy evening), perhaps she, who knows so many people, could find me employment, or a husband? I should think that a young, pretty, modest, industrious girl, for I have worked many times already, without telling of it, and the bread I have eaten in the morning I have often earned the previous evening, in an honest way, as I am now proving, since I might be rich by sacrificing my honesty (can you believe it? It is dreadful, mon Dieu!)—a girl, such as I am, ought to be worthy of a good man, even without a dowry. Now do with Iza as you please. I feel that I have no better friend than you, and you may be sure that no one loves you so much as your unhappy little wife,

Iza Dobronowska

"You are as good as God himself. I weep with joy and gratitude while writing you this last letter. Indeed you have loved me since the first day. And I loved you, thought of you all the time. It is our destiny, I see it clearly. Kiss your mother for me. I leave tomorrow; this evening, if I can. How anxious I am to see you. You shall know it all. I send you the longest lock of my hair, so if I should die on the way, you will have something of me, and you will know that I died thinking of you. From the moment you receive this letter, do not leave your studio, and have your key in the door. You will see it open suddenly, it will be me. What happiness! I love you! I love you! I love you! How glad I am at last that I can tell you. Thy little wife, this time for all time.

Iza

She was sincere when she wrote thus. Now, when I have so much to say against her, when I so much need her faults to offset mine, I swear it, she was not lying. She loved me. Do not doubt, my friend. She, like myself, came under the law of heredity, doubly indeed, since she was born of two completely vicious persons. The day following I received this:

"You have taken my child, monsieur. My incomparable child, for whom I have sacrificed so many years, and who recompenses me so badly. I hope you may be happy together, but I doubt it. Being an ingrate to her mother, she will be ungrateful to her husband. Iza takes with her all the papers necessary for her marriage, which I do not oppose, since I have nothing better to offer. Be assured, you will hear nothing further from me. I shall do my duty to the end. You will some day admit I was right, and you will regret the evil that you have done me. I have the honor to be,

Countess Dobronowska

I was careful not to show this letter, either to my mother or to M. Ritz; especially, as I had not taken them into my confidence as to my intentions in regard to Iza.

I was at this time in an exceptional pecuniary situation for an artist of my age. I could not supply all the demands for my work. I was earning thirty to forty thousand francs per year. I invested two-thirds of this, and we lived very well indeed, my mother and I, on the rest, accustomed as we both were to work, and to economical simplicity. Besides, I aspired to that independence which would permit me to dispose of my heart as I liked. I was robust, industrious, cheerful; I felt no limit to my strength. I had, therefore, no more doubt of the future than I had of the present, and I was even eager to take upon myself still another burden. I wished not only to owe everything myself, but I desired that others, and especially the wife whom I loved, should owe her livelihood and her happiness only to me.

Since Nature had given me talent, health, fortune, I considered that I had contracted a debt toward humanity, and I wished to share with those less fortunate than myself. I was often asked: "Why do you not marry? In your position you could make an excellent marriage; with your reputation, and your habits, you can, and ought to, have your choice. Enter some honorable family. Shall I find some one for you? etc." I declined all such offers. At first, I was unwilling, in the position I had made for myself, to submit my mother's past history to the investigations of any respectable family that might receive me in its bosom; afterward, I took pleasure in the thought which I will now explain.

As a poor girl, my mother had been betrayed, abandoned by a man; the poor girl who should become my wife, must be able to say that a man had taken her, without fortune, without protection, and that he had made her his happy and respected companion. This seemed to me the proper equilibration in the harmony of things, and to be consonant with that integrity which I had made the foundation of my life. Finally, with the love of an artist, an absurd love, a fatal love, call it what you please—I loved Iza.

She had taken possession of me through that first appearance at the ball, when by exquisite beauty, by the fear that I had suffered of losing her by my jealousy, by my regret, by that spontaneous appeal which the poor girl had made to my affection in beseeching me to remove her from the dangers which threatened her, by the need she had of me, by her poverty even, which was one cause of the withdrawal of vulgar men. Add to these reasons, the chastity in which I lived, and that need of loving, of telling it, of proving it, which belonged to my youth and which spurred me. Then one charm more: to love one in whom we can remember the child features, and ignore those of the woman, which our imagination perhaps depicts, carves, but cannot precisely know, nor translate, which one expects from moment to moment with all the impatience of the soul, which we feel approaching little by little from the air he breathes, which you hear coming with your heart, in whose arms you are about to throw yourself for your whole life. Was not that, indeed, the pure soul attraction which creates true love?

VII

I announced my intention to my mother, not so much with the view of consulting her, as to inform her of what was about to take place. For a long time she had refrained from seeking to influence me in any way, having found me far wiser in every respect than she had ever dared to hope. Everything I did was in her opinion well doné. She was pleased that I had never questioned about her life: she felt under obligation, therefore, not to scrutinize mine. My happiness was her prime mover. That I should take for a wife, a girl without fortune, seemed to her quite natural, as well as that all women should love me.

Besides, she had lived in such humble circumstances that many different possibilities were entirely outside of her suspicions. She had suffered wrong; but she had done none, consequently she did not foresee it. Perhaps, also, in seeing me gaining fame, she may have feared that an alliance with wealth might be the means of separating her from me. Any marriage, where she would be accepted, was agreeable to her.

She prepared the chamber for her daughter, as she already called Iza, and anticipated her coming with an impatience almost equal to mine own.

My friendship for, and gratitude to M. Ritz, remained the same. Our intercourse had become perforce less frequent. Apparently there was no change, and in that respect he deserved more credit than I. In fact, at each success I achieved, some of my admirers, who could not extol one without depreciating the other, availed themselves of the occasion to attack his works. It had been remarked many times that he was fortunate indeed to have produced such a pupil, as otherwise he would have accomplished nothing. This was unjust, but he did not permit himself to show that he felt the injustice. The more attention I bestowed, the more I sought to justify my rapid renown, the more humble I appeared in his presence, the more I threw him into the shade. My attitude toward M. Ritz became at times quite embarrassing. I owed everything to my protector, I was incapable of forgetting it, and I was debarred from giving advice or paying him a compliment for fear of wounding him; I showed him my studies; submitted my projects, and consulted him about my subjects. Several times I courted his criticism, appearing unable to complete my work without his help. When it was finished, and admired for any line or expression in which the old sculptor had assisted, I rejoiced to say in his presence:

"My master planned that, it is to him the compliment is due."

He pressed my hand at such times, and I felt he understood me, and that he had the nobility of soul to pardon me for my good intentions.

He lived with his daughter, his son-in-law, and their two children. In the bosom of his family he had nothing more to wish for. Constantin had gone to St. Cyr, and was already, what nature had always indicated that he would become, one of the best of officers in the African corps.

I corresponded with him, and, whenever he came to Paris, his second call was always upon me.

In the present circumstances, I felt I must confide my intentions to M. Ritz as well as to my mother. I told him my little romance, and the denoument that was about to follow.

"Is it a settled affair then," he asked, "or are you seeking advice?"

"It is a piece of news."

"Then, my dear boy," he said, kissing me, "accept my best wishes, and remember that my house is yours whether you are married or single."

"Will you do me the favor to be best man?" I asked.

"With the greatest pleasure," he replied.

Why did he not tell me all that he foresaw? But I should not have heeded him.

VIII

I t was noon on the second of March.

Iza entered my studio with noiseless step. I had left the key in the door as she had requested, and it made no sound.

Her face was concealed in a scarf of black lace, which, wrapped three times about her head, completely veiled her features from the most inquisitive eyes. She stood mute, motionless, impenetrable as the image of Destiny, holding with her two hands crossed upon her bosom, the flying ends of her curious veil. I looked at her a moment without being able to rise, so strongly did my heart beat. Then she loosened the scarf, took off her hat, and throwing both carelessly aside, exposed her bright face, which made the brilliancy of the mid-day light even more brilliant.

How was it that she was permitted to come so far to me? How could anybody avoid prostrating himself upon the way before this divine creature? Such grace, such splendid youth, these smiles, this intelligence, this soul, this beauty all for me! And these charms had been animated, developed at five hundred leagues' distance, for my happiness and for my genius. What a woman! I had done right to respect this love, and to keep myself pure for its coming. She knew her power full well, and seeing me thus overcome with admiration, she said in her child voice all unchanged:

"Do you find me beautiful?"

I ran to her, took her in my arms, raised her from the ground and covered her hair and hands with kisses.

"I have had this veil on my face for eight long days," she continued, pointing to her scarf; "I did not want any one to see me. I should have felt as if I were betraying you to reveal my countenance. You, also, you are beautiful, oh, so beautiful! How we shall love each other. And how delightful it is to be here. We will never go out. How good it is of you to marry me. What should I have done without you and your mother; where is she, that I may embrace her? Is my chamber ready? Now that I am all alone in the world, it is much more convenient to love you. Let us be married as soon as we can, shall we not? I have all my papers in order, here they are. They were prepared for the other one, Serge, you know. He had not the courage to oppose his family. Oh, at the last moment I should certainly have refused. What would I have become, since I love you? Quick, quick, my chamber; I am too tired to stand."

I called my mother. Iza threw herself on her neck with a filial embrace. My mother loved her at once, and led my fiancée to her little room, by the side of her own, above my studio.

"When I wake up," said Iza, "I will rap on the floor with my foot. Work on till then, monsieur." She kissed me on my forehead, and ran away to sleep till evening.

What a delightful life I led for the next two months, considerable time being required to comply with all the legalities. Iza went about the house as if she had been brought up there and never been away. She had the sprightliness of a bird. She would suddenly throw her arms around me and exclaim: "There are only so many more days to wait." Or, if she woke up in the night, she would strike the floor with the heel of her slipper and call out: "Good night, my dear." I always responded, for I slept but lightly. I thought of her incessantly. Love was supreme.

She told me all that had happened to her since we separated, and how my memory had always accompanied her during all the events.

Her mother had brought her to St. Petersburg in the hope that one of the princes would fall in love with her. She had not even been received at the palace; she had then taken her to all the public places until she was tired out. Upon her return to Warsaw she had tried to catch Serge in a snare, unknown to her daughter. They nearly had a lawsuit. There had been some plan about the theatre. Pushed to extremes by poverty, that woman had been willing to hand her over, let us say it, to sell her, to an immensely rich old man, who would assure her a fortune, and she had made this strange proposition to her daughter. After this confession, Iza no longer sought to conceal anything. She made me still another which fully confirmed me in the idea that we had been destined for each other from all eternity, and that there was already between us a mysterious and providential tie.

"Do you remember," she said one day, "when you first came to see us at the Quai de l'École. You looked at me closely. I asked why, because in your gaze there was something beside sympathy and friendship. You replied that you saw in me an extraordinary resemblance to one of your schoolmates named Minati, who had been dead several years. I immediately asked my mother in Polish, if I should tell you we had known the father of that youth. She replied 'No.' I therefore said nothing on the subject. Well I am the sister of André Minati. His father lived at Warsaw for three years. It seems that he was very handsome. He came often to my father's house before my birth. You see that I

ALEXANDRE DUMAS, FILS

have no secrets from you. Besides, what does it matter to you, but it is curious, isn't it?"

"Yes, very. How did you come to know the details?"

"When we were ruined, my mother appealed to M. Minati. I wrote the letters. He never replied. In a moment of anger, she let the secret escape before me, and afterward she told me all about it. Since that time we have learned of his death."

Fate played the cards in full sight; it was for me to decline, but I had no such thought.

I received two or three anonymous letters per week. They contained the strangest accusations, not only against the countess, but involving Iza herself. I showed them all to her, except those in which she would have been unable to comprehend the brutally technical expressions.

"This one must have come from Madame——, that from Madame——," said Iza, with the utmost tranquillity. "I am not angry with them, I am happy; but if you believe them, do not marry me. It is not too late. I will remain all the same with your mother. It is well for me to be here. I will not annoy you, and I will not cost you much. I will be your model if you wish it. It does not matter, provided I can see you. Do you want me for your mistress, in order to prove that I love you?"

"Don't speak in that manner;" I said, putting my hand upon her mouth. "She, who is to be my wife, must not talk thus."

"What do you mean?" she replied. "I know that a girl can live with a man without being his wife, and that she is dishonored in so doing; but I assure you I know nothing further, and I do not even know what the word means. If you love me and keep me with you, all the rest is of no importance to me."

The bans once published, there was much talk about the marriage, as everything made food for gossip, principally in our little circle of artists. This unexpected event gave opportunity for the most diverse comments. According to some I married a rich heiress whom I had abducted, to others it was an adventuress who had taken advantage of my well-known innocence. Some said Iza was a foreign princess in whom I had inspired a mad passion, and who had married me in spite of her parents' opposition; others intimated a model, who had for a long time followed the studios, and that many of her lovers could be named.

In Paris, the possessor of a name above the ordinary ranks is at the mercy of any newsmonger. Fortunately, Paris is a busy place and nothing, not even calumny, tarries long. In fact, Iza was unknown, invisible even, for I had not introduced her to any one before our marriage. It would have been futile to respect her as I did, if she was to be compromised by unveiling our life. We were never alone, and, when she was present at my work, my mother always joined us. I was too honest and too enamored to discount my happiness. I had to fight, however, against myself; for from the moment love takes possession of a nature so ardent and so long restrained as mine, it has a burning curiosity and fierce demands.

As we on the day of the ceremony entered the church, there was a rustle of admiration which turned to general applause, notwithstanding the sanctity of the place. You must remember that outburst, since you were present at the marriage. Adventuress or princess, respectable lady or grisette, Iza was to them all the most beautiful person they had ever seen, and they acknowledged the triumph of her youthful beauty, combined with a modesty that could not have been simulated. I was proud, I repeat, not only of being loved by so charming a being, but also of the act which I performed. My dream was realized; I had kept my word. I presented the rare and noble example of an honest man, industrious, celebrated, owing everything to his own efforts, marrying freely, without calculation or policy or marriage settlement, the woman of his choice, who would in turn owe everything to him, for whom he had preserved unsullied his heart and soul.

And this is why I married Iza. An act on my part absurd, but loyal and sincere.

IX

W e spent our honeymoon quite alone, in the country, at a cottage which had been placed at my disposal by the prince of R——. This little retreat was situated on the banks of the Seine, not far from Melun, at the foot of the St. Assise woods. It was taken care of in the winter by a gardener, his wife, and daughter, who were to provide for our material wants.

To be unknown, what joy! In the eyes of these honest people we were the friends of the prince, needing repose after a long journey. We thus escaped the inquisitiveness which pursues the newly married, no matter where they go, or however experienced they may try to appear. We had plenty of room, liberty, and our happiness all to ourselves. There we found the simplicity of country life combined with all the luxury and elegance of interior appointments. The liveried, cravated servant who returned in the summer with his master, had not yet entered upon his duties in these apartments hung with cashmere, chintz, or silk. Hardly did we hear the discreet step of the gardener's daughter performing, in the early morning, her housemaid's duties upon her tiptoes, that she might not awaken the distinguished guests, while the mother prepared for us that appetizing table which gardeners' wives so well understand.

Heart and stomach are such good neighbors in times of pure and healthful enjoyment; and then youth brightens what love ennobles.

It was nearly the 1st of May. O spring! Where is the man so unfavored by heaven as not to have listened, at least once in his life, to thy return from the depths? Who has not felt with joy the movement of the infant in the womb of earth, so full of promise, the coming summer? Have you never had in that indefinite period, especially if you were in love, a sense of dizziness that made you believe our sphere revolved more rapidly in order to sooner enjoy the kisses of her radiant spouse? And when the light clouds, the last fleeting vapors of winter are rudely torn, and reveal the blue sky, shining like a sapphire, soft as forgiveness, have you never distinctly seen God's smile, and felt yourself a better man? What a beautiful change in all nature. One burst of sunshine has proclaimed universal concert. He who wept, laughs; he who complained, smiles. The rain is cheerful; we no longer dread it; it only falls to bring forth flowers. If any belated flakes of snow fly about like the feathers of a pigeon, we watch them with mocking eyes, as masks at Lent. We light the fire and open the windows. Humanity seems about to enter at last into a definite contract with the rest of creation, that now is the end of evil, of doubt, of war, of suffering, and we are about to see the coming of an angel announcing the millennium.

That spring, what can give it back to me? We walked all day around those delightful little woods, almost untrodden, and the rambling paths led us, it mattered not where, and we kissed without disturbing even the birds, who knew it was the best of seasons for us as well as for them.

Those trees of St. Assise! I know them all and I love them still. It is not their fault that I am unhappy. They have not deceived me; they assisted in my happiness, and loaned me freely of their foliage and their shade for my first nest.

O Nature, so long as there shall remain one man upon earth, and a soul in that man, he will ask thee, as I do, what thou hast done with thy promises and his illusions? Why didst thou then smile? Why didst thou approve of me? Why didst thou seem to bless us with all thy voices, since at this hour, with no change of aspect, thou wilt not recognize me nor console me? Why, when unhappy, desperate, mad, I have come so loyally to thee, O Universal Mother, to ask counsel, encouragement, one smile, why hast thou not answered me, thou, whom I have known so eloquent and so generous? Ah! Thou hast already beheld the passage of myriads of lives, without changing or modifying thy immobile countenance. Of what account to thee is one anguish more or less?

One morning in May about ten o'clock, we were in the garden, near the river; Iza was lying upon one of those knotty bent willows by the water's edge, her hands clasped behind her neck; I was stretched out on the ground, kissing her little naked feet which she drew out, first one and then the other from the purple velvet slippers, to caress my face. Her long, rich golden hair was thrown carelessly back. Some long locks had escaped through the teeth of the large comb, like little cascades between the planks of a water-gate, and rolled down upon her dress and the bark of the willow. She wore only a blue cashmere wrapper, which I had caused to be made just like her garment of Quai de l'École, that I might have as much as possible before my eyes both the present and the past.

The graceful pose which she had taken, her wide sleeves falling back, exposed her white arms curved beside her head like the handles of an amphora. Her eyes blue as the sky they looked up to. Her beauty composed of the clearest tints. The gold of the harvest, the snow of the glaciers, the blue of the violets, roses, pomegranates, pearls; of these were her hair, her eyes, her cheeks, her lips, and her teeth, and all those blended in the harmony of youth, pleasure, and health. Aside from marble, alabaster, and pure wax, vainly would you search wherewith to compare that lovely, pliant form, known only to me, which her garments now hid, but whose wonderful contours my insatiable eyes divined. Not a human being for two leagues around. Only we two, and the smooth, deep water which flowed noiselessly. A splendid morning; an August morning wandered into May. By the inner quivering, which animated the silence, we could perceive that the country hastened to cover itself with green, as a young girl who has slept too long hurriedly puts on her most beautiful clothes that she may join her companions, who have already gone to the party.

The flowers, without being entirely unfolded, perfumed the air like those soul confessions which betray themselves in advance of the word. A transparent, opal haze, the last veil which the sun removes from the earth, ashamed to be surprised so soon, floated still upon the landscape, undulating all this luxury of life, converged toward us.

"What are you thinking of?" I asked softly.

"Do you love me?" she replied.

"A strange question."

"But very much, very much indeed?"

"More than words can tell."

"Then, go and bring me a large sheet, and some warm milk in a silver porringer with the prince's coat of arms on it."

I obeyed. In ten minutes I returned with the sheet folded on my arm and the porringer filled with milk, still smoking. Iza was no longer there. Her clothes were hung on a willow. I was thrilled with alarm. I stopped, not daring to take another step. My voice strangled in my throat. A burst of laughter responded to my fright.

"Hurry, I am enjoying myself."

The voice came from the river. Iza, entirely naked, swam in that icy water, splashing and beating it with her little feet, plunging, throwing back her hair like a veritable naiad, whose every grace she owned.

"You are insane," I cried. "You will kill yourself."

"No, I am used to this," she said.

"Suppose some one should see you?" I suggested.

"He would not be unfortunate. But don't be alarmed, nobody will see me, and besides, I have my hair."

"Come out, I beg of you."

"In one minute."

She plunged again, then swimming on the surface of the water to the shore, she seized a root, and with one bound sprang upon the bank, her head and shoulders covered with grasses which she pulled up as she came, and with which she adorned herself, with the instinctive grace that pervaded her simplest coquetries. I opened the sheet to envelop her. "No, the milk first," she said, and seizing the bowl, she began to drink slowly, all moist and rosy, with little swallows, her head bent forward, her loins a little curved, saying:

"Look, a subject for a statue. Isn't it pretty?"

She emptied the bowl to the last drop, then threw it upon the grass at the risk of denting it.

"What if you had spoiled this piece of silver," I remarked, in a tone of gentle reproach.

"What if I had?" she laughed, "it isn't mine."

That was the first word upon her lips which shocked me. I might then have learned her character from it. I have recalled it many times—too late. When I had taken the grasses from her hair, and covered her with the sheet, there was not a drop of water on her whole body, the heat of her blood had dried her skin.

"See how warm I am," said she. And in fact from her body rose a light, fragrant vapor.

"You will not do such a foolish thing again, dear," I begged while helping her to dress, and I looked around to see if any one observed us, but nobody was in sight. She replied:

"If you only knew how nice it is to be in the water. For more than an hour I have had these three desires, to undress myself, to plunge into the water, and to drink milk from a silver bowl. If I had asked your advice, you would certainly have opposed me, so I did it without saying anything about it."

And, leaping upon my neck, she folded me in her arms and held out her rosy lips flecked with milk.

ALEXANDRE DUMAS, FILS

X

I relate this scene in all its details, because it contains the germs of the three vices which were to ruin this woman, and afterward myself: immodesty, ingratitude, sensuality. However, aside from the surprise which her reply in the matter of the porringer caused me, this adventure left upon my mind only a picture of love and innocent playfulness. Iza repeated the prank, or rather we played it together, several times, for I wished to share in all her sensations. She called me Daphne, I called her Chloe, and after a while I found this mythological bath quite natural, though since polite society came into existence, the line has been drawn.

There would have been but little harm in these secluded sports had we gone no further, but the love which I inspired in Iza, was essentially physical. She at that time had no more doubt of its innocency than I, and as the holy bond of wedlock which united us, gave her the right to know and to enjoy all the privileges of marriage, she did not shrink from its material pleasures.

Just here is the place for a delicate statement. The bill of indictment will doubtless charge, as Iza has repeated many times since our separation, in order to exculpate herself, that I used my wife for a model. I shall be reproached for having demoralized the young girl of whom the law gave me full ownership, and whose innocence and moral purity I should have guarded.

The first point is true, the second false. Alas, the demoralization was instinctive, vice was natural to that virgin; and if either was demoralized by the other, it was the man.

Yes, I was born with all the physical appetites and the more I had immolated them before marriage upon the altar of my profession and my ideal, when the ideal was incarnated, the marriage consummated, the less I purposed to limit and restrain these appetites, and least of all when I found in my wife the same thirst to gratify them. Therefore neither of us were to blame. I was twenty-six, Iza eighteen. She was Beauty, I Power, and we loved each other.

I will tell you, however, since you have become my confessor, that my first sentiment, when I had obtained the right to remove the veil from this divine creation, were those of admiration and respect, more than desire. Such is the effect of supreme Beauty. It exalts the mind, and saturates the soul before it appeals to the senses. In his admirable picture of Venus and Adonis, Prudhon has translated this impression with the delicacy of a real poet, and real lover. The most beautiful of the Olympian divinities, entirely nude, and absolutely feminine, offers herself to the kisses and caresses of one of the most perfect of mortals. He gazes upon her with rapture but does not dare, either with hands or lips, to touch that celestial form. I had experienced that emotion, but little by little it had given place to a more human feeling. Nevertheless for a long time I remained modest under all circumstances, and I should have continued so, had I obeyed my own impulses. Unfortunately, Iza, though reserved and modest before strangers, when with me knew no shame whatever. Proud of her beauty, she lavished it upon me at the slightest pretext, and constantly, and the scene of the bath is but one of a thousand tableaux that she delighted to offer me.

Nor was this all. When she exclaimed that May morning while drinking: "Here is a statue already made," she returned for the twentieth time perhaps since our marriage to her fixed idea, of seeing represented and immortalized in marble the body whose grace and symmetry ravished me, both as husband and artist. She did not have to plead long to gain her point. Stronger men than I would have yielded. For an artist loving his art, and possessing a wife whom he adores as its most perfect embodiment, and these two loves being fused, it would indeed be difficult, perhaps even beyond the power of man to refuse. I appeal to the sincerity of the sex, if there does exist a sincere woman. Where is there one, endowed with love and beauty, such as Iza found herself, who would not have felt the same ambition?

"Seeing that I love you, and that I am jealous of all women, and since you find me more beautiful than any," she said, "and as my beauty may be useful to you in your art, let me serve your fame as I do your pleasure, so I may, at all times be a part of your life. I would not that you should be happy, nor even inspired, without me. I shall grow old. You will need some evidence that I was once beautiful. And, if I should die tomorrow, what would remain of your Iza? When memory shall fade, the marble will endure. Are you not willing that we should go down to posterity as we have gone through life, together? It is not Chance, believe me, who has given, as companion and lover, a beautiful girl to a great artist, it is Destiny. Finally, the best reason of all, it will make me happy."

What could be my answer to such arguments?

XI

The first statue I made, with Iza for a model, was *La Buveuse*, for which she gave me the motiv at St. Assise, and which is only known to the public as a statuette. You remember the great success it obtained. I refused to sell it at any price, and I would not even show it to any one, except to M. Ritz and my mother. It was life size and I placed it, as an eternal memento of happy days, between the two windows of our nuptial chamber. It is the exact reproduction of Iza, of whom I made a cast from head to foot, one night with the doors securely closed. To avert suspicion, I afterward employed a model, the celebrated Aurélie, but in fact, I only worked after the cast, which I have destroyed, and also the only figure I took from it. I regret this now, for Art might have profited by that beauty which was to do so much harm.

I realized the dream of Pygmalion. She, whom I loved, became woman and statue, alternately. However, as I feared our secret would be discovered, I changed the dimensions. My success increased, no doubt, but my worth certainly diminished. I turned aside from the ideal of pure art. I degraded it to the narrow proportions of the popular taste. Mastered by love and by the senses, in spite of myself I entered into the sensualistic school. I could not supply the demand for my work. I limited my productions, against the advice of Iza, who was eager for wealth and luxury. My mother took charge of the house, which my wife very cheerfully surrendered to her. To be beautiful, to hear me say it, to love me, and to furnish plastic studies, for which she had a genius, this was all she knew or cared for. My talent was now largely concentrated in her. If I had lost her at this period, I should have died of grief, as did the author of Venus and Adonis after the suicide of his mistress, for it frequently happens that artists are killed by women. Unfaithful, she kills Giorgious; for love she kills Raphael; dead, she kills Prudhon.

It became evident that, notwithstanding the precautions which we had taken, the truth was suspected, and among the amateurs who came, more than one doubtless bought the image of the beautiful person who sometimes did the honors of the studio. I thus profited unwittingly by a curiosity which brought discredit upon me, and what was still more foreign to my thought, Iza could derive pleasure from this traffic. She had wished me to make, for sale in the shops, a statuette of La Buveuse, and this incognito she enjoyed,—exposure of herself, for the admiration of the public. When we went out together in the evening she would stop before a shop window in which were copies of La Buveuse or of Daphne, and whisper to me, in the midst of the gazing crowd: "They don't suspect that it is me." She delighted to excite desire and enjoyed the insolent homage rendered to the bronze or marble which represented her. This was only the unfaithfulness of mind, but it was unfaithfulness. However, she never left me a moment, and even when we had visitors she scarcely moderated her expressions of tenderness. She affected to be my slave, my chattel; she desired to have it known that she adored me, and that she was unapproachable. Indeed, no one could have dressed more modestly than Iza, in her long loose-fitting white gown, which covered everything but her hands, her feet, and her head. This affectation of modesty in all her person foiled the revelations of art, and made it impossible for the inquisitive to affirm any positive resemblance to this woman already in pursuit of eccentricity.

Vice has its innocence and artlessness. There are beings created to do evil, who have the instinct, the necessity, and who follow it without premeditation or consciousness, as the serpent kills, or as the lotus destroys reason. Iza was one of these creatures, and at this period, the first year of our marriage, she was ignorant whither these primitive inclinations would lead.

In the mean while I was perfectly happy with my wife, my work, and my mother. What more could I wish for? A child perhaps? It did not come; as if nature hesitated, either through fear of destroying one of her most perfect works by breaking the harmonious lines of that beautiful body while giving passage to another life, or perhaps she reserved maternity as a punishment for such a creature.

Iza, in fact, dreaded this possible event; she was afraid of the dangers and devastations it would bring. As to myself, I had suffered so much in my childhood that although my own offspring might not have to endure the same, I was indifferent. My mother, however, wished it. Did she look upon the happiness of my son as a compensation for the sufferings of her own? Did she look farther into the future than I? Did she count upon that birth to modify the character of her daughter-in-law whose tendencies could not have escaped her observation?

We had plenty of time, I said, when she broached the subject to me; Iza is so young. Let her remain a child herself a few years longer. Besides, it is Nature's business, not mine.

XII

Men who live by their brains, scholars, musicians, writers, painters, sculptors seldom become fathers. To those whom God has enriched with the gift of intellectual procreation, has been given but incidentally the faculty of physical generation. Such men often love the children of others more than they would have loved their own. Sometimes they have a hatred for those they have begotten,—of these unnatural fathers Jean Jaques Rousseau is a remarkable type.

Now, this strange phenomenon is perfectly explicable; I can assert it since I have experienced it myself. Let us confess: Genius is absorbent and egotistical. It asks nothing better than to be propagated, but in a manner suiting its caprice. It abhors all that enchains it, and everything that assimilates it to other men; all that trammels its development, and restrains its flight. The family, as it has been constituted by society, is one of the fetters, therefore nearly all great men have evaded the obligation, or sacrificed it, and the wives of husbands who are truly illustrious, must surrender many illusions and tender hopes. Those who choose to live with lions, must take the chance of being devoured by them.

And this is the excuse of genius, if any apology be needed, for it is only responsible to heaven, and should not be judged by the rules and regulations which govern ordinary humanity. To beget a child is doubtless the culmination of man's power; by that act he comes nearest to Deity. In the love of a father, pride dominates. "It is I who have given life to this little being," is his thought when he regards and admires his babe. But he has not engendered that life without the aid of woman, and she is more mother of the child, than the man is father. Very often, the parents are jealous of what they owe to each other, in this joint production, and instead of "Our son," "Our daughter," they say "My son," "My daughter," as if seeking to create a private interest in this indivisible estate. But the property is perishable, tending inevitably to destruction, and the pleasure which it gives may change at any moment into unavailing and eternal regret. How different a pride, and how much greater should, therefore, a man feel in the work of his mind, which emanates from himself alone, and contains within itself the principle of eternity. It makes illustrious him who has conceived it, and carries his name across the ages, forming a part of that indestructible, though imaginary world, which human thought has created beside the real to console us for the latter. This child, the issue, not of a secretion from the blood, but of all purest emotions of the soul, meditation, fancy, perseverance, anguish sometimes, will be a companion, a friend for myriads, for humanity entire when once realized.

Behold the divine creators, Mahomet, Homer, Virgil, Dante, Shakspeare, Raphael, Columbus, Galileo, Michael Angelo, Molière, Pascal, Montaigne, Mozart, Voltaire, Newton. What emotion comparable to that of spiritual parturition could come to these men from the bringing into the world of a helpless, wailing infant, which the meanest hod-carrier could engender as well as themselves? Shall he confine himself to the family, this seeker to whom the whole visible world does not suffice? Shall he concentrate his adoration upon an atom, this giant who would scale heaven? Should he desert the boundless kingdom of ideas for the narrow domain of the sentiments? No! Jesus himself was forced to choose, and, to prove that he was God, be neither son, nor husband, nor lover, nor father. And he has given birth to the grandest idea of the ages.

XIII

B ut I have wandered far from myself. This reasoning, made in the name of men of genius, is in no way applicable to me. They would simply recognize me as a poor man of talent whom passion has struck to earth. However, for a long time I thought I had mustered in their ranks, but in placing passion above art, I separated myself from them. I should not have loved, or should asked of love only inspiration or pleasure. For lofty spirits, passion should be but a motive power, as the wind to the sea; it lifts it, makes it wild and magnificent, then disappears,—and the sea remains.

I no longer saw save with Iza's eyes. She dreaded to have a child.

So I was dismayed when she announced with an expression of anger that she was *enceinte*. All the imprudent things which might do away with that condition she had already tried, before saying anything to me. There was no alternative. She must be a mother. She did not dare to propose a crime, but she had considered it, I am sure.

She spent all her days and nights in weeping. I tried to comfort her, telling her she would remain beautiful notwithstanding, and that tears and sleepless nights would disfigure her more than the natural accident. It would be better to become resigned, and to take all the precautions which would enable her to bring forth this life without any loss to herself. She was, besides, one of those fortunate creatures, especially constructed for love, so supple, so elastic, on whom maternity leaves hardly a trace.

I would not permit her to walk; I carried her and watched her constantly. I designed and modelled children, angels, cupids, with little fat hands and rubicund faces, with dimpled thighs and chubby bellies, and I surrounded Iza with these, as a Greek artist would have done, in order that the mother should conceive the Beautiful.

At this time she talked about her possible death. She had great fear of it; she shuddered at the idea of the cold, wet earth. She exacted from me a promise that I would not marry again, and that I would go to the cemetery every day; she must be dressed in lace and covered with flowers. I should carve her statue, life size, in marble, and place it above the grave, that her beauty might survive and interpret for a moment the sorrow of those who might pass near it. She had, in fine, all the cowardice, and therewith all the charm of womanhood.

Since our marriage Iza had corresponded but rarely with her mother; her pregnancy caused this correspondence to become more frequent. I do not need to tell you that I supplied the needs of the countess, whom the injustice and the ingratitude of the Czar left continually in poverty.

One day Iza told me that her mother desired to assist at her confinement, and she would be filled with remorse if she died without seeing her.

Be merciful to sinners! I sent the countess the money necessary for the journey. She came. She wept, threw herself upon my neck, kissed my hands, explained, minimized the facts, ended the misunderstanding between my wife and myself. She called me her son, and installed herself in our house, spending her whole time near her daughter, conversing with her only in Polish, and frequently I surprised Iza paying the deepest attention to the maternal recitals. I asked her the nature of these conversations which appeared so interesting. She told me whatever she chose.

A man who marries a foreigner, and who does not understand his wife's tongue, has but one thing to do, learn that language as quickly as possible, and unknown to his wife.

On the thirteenth of April, four years ago at midnight, Iza brought into the world that son, for whose sake I am seeking today to exonerate myself, and to live.

The child was intrusted to my mother and a nurse, for Iza refused to nourish it. She had but one care since her deliverance; to obviate the traces of her pregnancy. She saw her son about half an hour each day and the rest of the time thought no more about him. My mother proposed to go to the country with the child and nurse. The fresh air would be good for the baby, she said, and the little one could not yet be very interesting to us. It was evident that my poor mother had not come to a good understanding with the countess, and she would prefer to go away, rather than have me know of their discussions. I did not then comprehend the gravity of the condition. The countess appeared to me rather foolish, but what did it matter? I was beloved, and she was the mother of Iza! She had had bad schemes: Love had baffled them. I saw in her only a woman who threw herself upon our resources, and I was so happy that I could have pardoned almost anything.

I consulted Iza as to my mother's proposal. She disapproved, adding, as though she divined the real cause for her departure:

"It is unnecessary, my mother will soon be going away." In fact, the countess did take leave, her business (that interminable business!) again calling her to Poland.

One month after her confinement Iza was about, more beautiful than ever. I now lived almost entirely in my family. During the winter I had two or three big parties in my studio. Every week I gave a dinner to some of the distinguished men of Paris. You, too, occasionally did me the favor to be one of us, and you may remember what these reunions were, on the surface at least, for God only knows what lurked beneath.

I hired, at Auteuil, a small house for the summer with a fine garden and a great out-building, which I converted into a studio. We moved there in the spring, and I never left it except for such work as required my presence in the city. Iza seemed to accustom herself to the rôle of mother. If she did not worship Felix, at any rate he amused her; he would doubtless interest her later.

Her maternity seemed to have made her more chaste and modest, even in our intimacy. This new sensation had revealed to her some new duties; at least she said so. There was no longer the question of utilizing her beauty, and I could receive any number of models, without exciting her jealousy at all. She even blushed at having lent herself to these fantasies of art. I must ascribe that compliance to passion, and to ignorance and youth. I loved her a thousand times more when she spoke in this way. She was more affectionate to my mother than I had ever seen her. Oh, how well she played her game. Who could have anticipated the future, in seeing her roll with her baby in the sweet new-mown hay on one of those pleasant June evenings, while I, lying upon the grass, my whole nature in a melting mood, could scarcely contain myself for happiness.

XIV

Autumn approaching, I received a letter from the countess, which notified me of her decision to return to Paris and to settle herself permanently. She thanked me for my hospitality, and reimbursed the money which I had furnished her. All the suits were settled. She had at last come into possession of a considerable sum; she should avail herself of this income to remain near her daughter, and she could now manage without any expense to me. She did not propose to live with us; did not want to annoy us; but, she would like to be in the same city with her dear children. She would consider it a pleasure to assist my mother in caring for the little one.

She came, and hired a small house on the Avenue Marbeuf; we were then living in the large house in the Rue de Bemy, No. 71, and therefore neighbors. Iza went to see her mother nearly every day, with nurse and baby. Frequently I accompanied them, or called to bring them home. The countess dined with us whenever she chose. On these occasions she brought her needlework, or sewed for her grandson. This was grandmotherly. She had abandoned the struggle to appear young, had accepted the situation gracefully and let nature have its own way with her gray hairs. She had enough to live well, the future was assured, she could love us without being suspected of calculation. She asked nothing more of heaven. Our happiest evenings were spent in this manner: I designing or modelling, my mother putting her grandchild to sleep, the countess embroidering and telling stories; Iza playing, singing, laughing, eating bonbons.

However, my mother became all at once very depressed. Several times I saw that her eyelids were red. I asked her the cause of this sadness; she denied it: age, her idle life; she was, perhaps, too happy. She had always worked. It was no doubt the change which affected her.

My relations with M. Ritz grew less and less intimate. A diseased liver had made him a hypochondriac, and compelled him to lead a sedentary life; he lived entirely with his daughter and son-in-law. He treated me no longer as his child. Iza attributed this change to jealousy; the pupil overshadowed too much the master. That was possible. Nor did his daughter enjoy Iza's visits. Iza was prettier, more elegant, had more admirers, held a more desirable position than Madame Niederfeld. Female rivalry, why not? They remained perfectly polite to each other,

ALEXANDRE DUMAS, FILS

returning their calls of twenty minutes each on the proper days, but nothing more. This attitude of M. Ritz and his daughter should have opened my eyes, but I saw nothing. My wife's explanation seemed to me sufficient.

With Constantin it was quite different. He had served in several campaigns in Africa, and, having been wounded and decorated, he returned to France as aide-de-camp of the Minister of War. He led a gay life. However, upon his return he had the habit of coming frequently to our house, after a while his visits became fewer, and finally ceased altogether. When we met by chance, and I expressed my surprise and regret for his neglect, he merely pressed my hand and made some commonplace excuse. The last time that I saw him, previous to the great events which were preparing, he said to me, as if he had a prevision of their imminence: "You are really one of those men whom I love and esteem very much; but you know we can't always do as we would like. Some day, however, if you need a true friend count on me. I am one of those who are more real than apparent."

I told Iza of this remark, though without giving it any special significance. She replied by one of those semi-confidential smiles, as if to say: "I know all about it, that isn't it." I pressed her for an explanation.

"Promise me upon your honor," she said, "that you will not discuss it with any one, not even your mother, and especially that you will say nothing to Constantin."

I promised faithfully.

"And that what I tell you, will not change your manner toward him?"

"Not in the least."

"Upon your honor?"

"Upon my honor."

"Very well; Constantin has been very attentive to me, and he does not come here any more for the reason that I have asked him to stay away. I have not mentioned it to you, because it is not worth while to trouble one's husband with such matters. A woman who respects herself, can make others respect her. At present it is quite unimportant, and I can tell you everything. You believe in your friend, you believe him to be good and true. I don't think so. I consider him capable of taking a mean revenge. Has he never told you anything to my discredit?"

"Never."

"I am surprised; he will do it. Oh, these men who are wounded in their self-complacency, we women know them. I have your promise?"

"Rest easy, I shall not say anything." But I felt from that moment a hatred for my old friend, and had I met him that day I should certainly have insulted him. This was the first of those premonitions, which I let pass without notice, and which later rose up before my face, and, removing their masks, called me an imbecile. I should have divined it then.

Another time, Iza said: "I have a confession to make and a pardon to ask for."

"What is it?"

"My bust, which you had made when I was sixteen, and which you sent to Poland."

"Yes, what of it?"

"It remained there in pledge with many more of our things."

"Which I offered to redeem a number of times."

"My mother did not want to increase her obligations to you, and therefore declined your offers at the time of her last visit. She was unable to see the party who had loaned us the money on these things. He was away from home. He is a Jew in the usury trade. Mother left the amount due, with one of her friends, and they are in possession of the bust. Instead of having it brought here, I have sent it to my sister. Did I do wrong?"

"You did quite right, dear child."

"It is my own sister, and she has always been as obliging to us as she could be. You are not vexed about it?"

"What a foolish question."

Two months later, on her birthday, Iza mentioned:

"Do you know that I made a good investment unconsciously in sending that bust to my sister? See this!"

She opened a jewel case which contained a necklace of diamonds and emeralds worth from thirty to forty thousand francs.

"And your sister sent that jewelry?"

"Who else do you think? Here is her letter. She is lovely."

"This present is so valuable, it embarrasses me."

"Don't have any scruples, sister is rich and vain. When I was only a poor little girl she made me presents; now that I am the wife of a distinguished man, she is proud of me. It seems that you are even more celebrated in Russia than in France. Besides, she has done it handsomely. This jewel comes from the Magasin Anglais, Newski Perspective," and she showed me the card of the establishment in golden letters on the white satin of the case.

Then she read her sister's letter, full of thanks and compliments for me.

"Well, I will give you the ear-rings to match," said the countess, who was present at this conversation.

"But mamma, ear-rings in emeralds and diamonds to match these, would be an affair of ten or twelve thousand francs, nearly a whole year of your revenue."

"There is the Starckau estate coming back to me."

"Indeed."

"And for which I already have a purchaser. All the money is for thee, my dear daughter; for you, my dear children; what difference does it make whether I give it to you in diamonds or in gold?"

Wishing to lessen our obligation in the matter, I offered Iza's sister a marble, which Iza took upon herself to forward to her.

Six weeks later, on returning from a promenade with her mother, nurse, and baby, Iza remarked in the most natural tone:

"Who do you think we met today?"

"I can't guess."

"Try?"

"Somebody that I know?"

"Only by name, but you ought not to have forgotten that name."

I mentioned several people.

"You will have to give it up."

She gave me plenty of time, and with the air of a happy child, whose puzzle nobody could guess, said:

"Serge!"

I turned pale, not having, however, the slightest suspicion, without the least presentiment even; but this Serge was the only man who had ever troubled my mind, and I heard the name with a shudder.

"Did he speak to you?" I asked.

"Yes. If you had seen his face you would have been awfully amused. A man, who cannot possibly live without you, who must kill himself if you don't marry him, and then you meet him soon after, looking in the very best of health. I could not restrain myself from laughing in his face. But he had the good taste not to allude to the past."

"You have not invited him to call on us, I trust?"

"No; but he can come or stay away, and it will be all the same. Have I done wrong to tell you about this encounter? Do you want me to keep any secrets from you? You need only say so."

"You have done right. Kiss me."

And she gossiped about the promenade, her little purchases, the weather, and of the crowd in the streets.

About a month after this scene, I arrived at home quite unexpectedly. While opening the parlor door I heard Iza's voice; it was at an unusual pitch.

"What a torment she is!"

"Of whom are you speaking?" I asked, as I entered.

"We were talking about the chambermaid," explained the countess.

"But, dear child," I remonstrated, "one in your position should not speak so, even of a servant; what is wrong with her?"

"Nothing serious; but I am feeling badly today. Your mother, too, is suffering."

"My mother. Has she gone to bed?"

"No, she complains of headache."

"Why are you not with her?"

"She prefers to be alone."

I went to mother's room, and found her pale and greatly agitated. She had certainly been weeping, and was ready to weep again when she saw me. It required all the strength of such a will as hers to remain mistress of her feelings.

"Iza tells me that you are sick."

"It is no matter, my child, only a pain in the head."

"You have been weeping."

"Yes, the suffering was, for a little while, intense."

"Why do you prefer to be alone?"

"Because the slightest noise unnerves me."

"Have you any complaints to make of any one, here?"

"Oh, no!"

She was unable to contain herself longer, and throwing her arms about me, burst into tears. I began to be alarmed.

"There is something wrong, tell me."

"Oh, nothing."

"Some accident to baby?"

"Baby is well; no, I assure you, it is I who have been out of sorts. For some time I have been unwell, but seeing you, I am better. Let us go down to the parlor."

She was calm all the evening. For eight days I stayed in the house and during this time, she, my wife, and the countess were the best of friends. But mother changed perceptibly, growing weaker day by day. I consulted a doctor, one of my friends, and asked him to disclose the trouble. "She has hypertrophy of the heart; a disease that afflicts those who have loved too much, worked too hard, or endured a great deal. It is an evil of long standing, and cannot now be cured, only watched. Above everything she must avoid all strong emotions."

I leave you to imagine how this news affected me. I remained constantly with mother, who knew the truth about herself.

If it were only the matter of dying, she would have accepted death without fear. To die is nothing for those who have struggled much, it is only the last struggle. But she was aware of the intrigues which surrounded me, and of which I had no suspicion, and concerning which she desired I should continue ignorant, for fear the revelation would kill me. While she remained near me, she could throw herself between me and my fate, be my refuge, strengthen and console me, if the truth came to light. With her dead, what would happen when the great calamity should come? This was the constant thought of her, to whom all emotion was forbidden.

Nothing uses up life faster than to nurse a secret, which, a thousand times a day, flashes from the brain to the lips, then falls with all its weight upon the heart. Happily, my mother had one confidant, Constantin, to whom she commended me and who told me later all she had said. She went to see him when able, but he only came to the house when she was confined to her room. I felt grateful to him for these visits and my resentment was in some degree weakened thereby. Still Iza's revelation stood between us always.

"You have no better friend in the world than Constantin," said my mother. "Promise me if any of those troubles which it is well to provide for in happy days, in these days especially, should materialize, then confide your child to his sister. Do not forget you owe to that family what you are. All our happiness came from them. Beware of ingratitude, so common to success."

Iza took care of the invalid with every appearance of sincerity; but home-life became very hateful to her. She was evidently tired of it. I gave her all the variety I could. My mother insisted upon it; though it was with great reluctance that I left her bedside, in order to accompany Iza to the theatre and other places of amusement. Frequently I let her go with the countess, and to my great surprise she was perfectly willing to do without me. I felt that she ought to remain and share my fears and anxiety. But she was so young. I always had this good excuse ready. Two or three times, mother, feeling her end near, had long private conversations with my wife, who then appeared much disturbed.

"Spare me these scenes," Iza said to me one day; "they are very distressing."

She was now bed-ridden, the latest symptoms gave no hope. Of all the ways of leaving this world, heart disease is the worst, painful for those who suffer, and for those who see them suffer.

"Is there nothing that can save her?" I asked the doctor.

"A miracle," he answered with the sad smile of unavailing science.

That day I remained for two hours in a church. I do not know what I said to God, what exchange I offered of my fame, my wealth, my happiness, for the life of my mother, but never, certainly, has a human creature implored heaven with more humility. God made no answer.

"My dear son," spoke the sweet and brave invalid the evening of her death, "except for having brought thee into the world under bad conditions, I have nothing to reproach myself. Since thy birth, I have had no care except for thy happiness, and I go hence without fear, and without remorse. The benediction of the one who has loved thee more than any other upon earth, I say with confidence, is able to preserve thee during the time that thou hast still to live. I give it thee from the bottom of my heart. I have the right to bless, at this supreme moment. The sins that I have committed, I have expiated. I have in evidence of this expiation, the love and respect of my son and the happiness that he has given me, for there has never, never been a happier mother than thine, remember that, and let it be thy consolation when she shall be no longer with thee. I have many times asked myself whether, before dying, I should reveal to thee the secret which has lain so long upon my heart. What could it avail thee? Forgive, my child, even without knowing what thou art forgiving. We are all weak creatures, none can answer for himself; and when the hour comes, which I feel already approaching, we are stronger in proportion as we have been merciful. I leave thee in the fulness of thy talent, thy fame, and thy wealth; between thy wife and thy son whom thou lovest, and who will occupy the place that I leave vacant. It is the law of nature, do not refuse this consolation, do not forget me too soon. It is all that I ask. I have been all my life but an ignorant woman, yet I affirm to thee that there is another world and that we shall find each other there. Kiss me; do not leave me till the end, and let me feel thee, even when I cannot see thee."

She asked for the priest. At five o'clock the next morning she died, after a long struggle, and departed, taking with her the secret which had hastened her death.

When I saw, motionless and cold, that mother who had been so long the sole occupant of my heart and my thought, it seemed as though I should sink like an inert and henceforth useless mass. So the end came. Those joys, those kisses, those tendernesses, those numberless sacrifices, the unceasing devotion, our happy hours, our times of sadness, the laughter and the tears of former days, the memories and the realities, the hopes and promises for the future—all past. One last breath had borne them all away. Strangers, animals alive, and my mother dead. It cannot be. I am not myself, or else I dream.

XV

I sincerely believed I had become acquainted with the greatest of human griefs. Iza wept vehemently; a purely physical emotion which is the special privilege of women. They are afraid in the dark. On the morrow they think no more about it. I was touched, and received great consolation from these facile tears.

But for six months I could not smile, neither upon her nor upon my child. My mother's form would appear before my eyes; some scene, some word from the past would enter my mind, and with a sob I would kiss Iza's hands, and remain for hours without speaking a word.

I worked furiously. I began to save up money for my son, for whom, had I died at that time, I should have left but little. We had been spending all I earned. Death made me see life in its serious aspect, imposing upon me duties beyond this world. Renown, talent, even love, all at once appeared to me as temporary possessions. My soul was filled with religious thoughts. If I had been alone, ART would not have sufficed to console me; I should, probably, have retired to some monastery, an idea, which, with wife and child, I could not entertain. I plunged into symbolic art. For a whole year, I was an artist of the middle ages. It was then I carved the statue of *Saint Félicité*, according to the legend, as nursing her child while going to her punishment, and to whom I gave my mother's features, whose patron saint she was.

Thus, like a true artist, I utilized my grief and wore it out. Little by little it vanished, until I saw it only as vapor floating in a sky which had again become blue. Insensibly familiarized with this emotion, I heard it only as a sad undertone in the noise and commotion of life around me. At last I found myself laughing, as if my mother had been with me.

Poor human nature!

Iza had wished to wear mourning as long as I did.

"Let me continue in it," she said. "I owe your mother that much." I would not permit it, and at the end of six months she returned to her usual attire.

One morning, I received an anonymous letter. I submit to you its contents:

"You are a remarkable husband; you do not perceive that your wife goes out every morning and runs about the streets, when you think she is quiet in her room. Follow her, and you will learn some news: but do not show her this letter, and betray nothing.

A Friend

Say what you will about an anonymous missive, it never fails to have some effect. It is an abominable weapon, unfair, infamous, but it is sure.

I concealed my feelings, as well as I could, all the rest of the day. Twenty times I was on the point of showing the letter to Iza, and demanding to know the truth, but I restrained myself.

On the morrow I dressed early, and, hidden behind the curtains of my window, I watched for this mysterious exit.

About eight o'clock Iza, veiled, in black dress, went out, looking about to see if any one was observing her. You may imagine my heart beat at this sight. She hailed a passing carriage. I made one bound to the street. I could have recognized that vehicle among a thousand; I soon overtook and followed it. Passing through the outer Boulevard it approached the cemetery Montmartre. Iza descended, and entered the burial grounds. The gardener saluted her as an habitual visitor, and accompanied her, with flowers, to my mother's grave, which I had not visited for several days. She kneeled, and placed the floral offerings upon the mound; then returned home by the same route and with the same precautions. Humiliated, I fell upon her neck, and showing the anonymous note, asked her pardon.

"Ah, the confidence of a man who loves us!" she sighed.

From that day, whenever she went out, clad in black, I kissed her and pressed her hand, but never questioned where she was going.

XVI

M. de Merfi, one of the best known amateurs in Paris, owner of a large country seat near Chartres, had invited me to the opening of the sporting season. I responded affirmatively and was to leave home at six o'clock on the morning of August 30th.

I had accepted, as one often does this sort of invitation, through mere politeness, saying to myself: "It is so far off, something or other will intervene."

However, on the 29th of August I looked at my valise, which Iza had packed with all the care of a good wife, and inspected my gun in its leather sheath.

"I have decided to remain home," I said suddenly, "and will write to M. de Merfi at once."

"But," interposed Iza, "it is too late."

"Only ten o'clock, and he never retires till midnight."

"You would enjoy yourself very much, I am sure."

"No, I am not going."

"It would do you good, and when you get there, you will be glad you went."

"No, I will send a note."

"I think the servant has gone to bed. You said you wouldn't need him, and to call you at five o'clock."

"Ring for him," I insisted, while saying to myself: "If the fellow is asleep, I will go to the hunt."

Such is fate. If the man had been in his bed, my position would doubtless be entirely different today.

He was awake. I handed him the letter for M. de Merfi excusing my absence by the statement, that I was compelled to finish an important piece in forty-eight hours. The great heat might dry the clay and spoil it, if I left it for three days. Anticipating that M. de Merfi might perhaps call to press me, I resolved to verify my apology by a couple of hours of work.

"All right," said Iza pleasantly. "Work away, and if your friend comes, my word for it, you will join in the hunt tomorrow. You haven't the heart to disappoint the poor man."

"Well, should he persist, I will go."

With eased conscience, I began to sketch the subject which I proposed to commence upon at daybreak. I labored in silence, showing my drawing to Iza, who kissed me, as she stooped to inspect it.

No one came. At midnight I repaired to my chamber. Iza went to her own. I slept but little, awoke early, and started to work without making any noise.

XVII

I t was nearly six o'clock when Iza gently opened the door of her room. I have already told you that her boudoir opened into my studio. In the position I occupied, behind a large group, Iza could not see me. But I could see her in a small mirror hung at my left, a little inclined, which reflected all the parts of the room. Her hair undone, with a chemise slipping down oyer her shoulders and only one skirt, she advanced upon the tips of her little bare feet, holding up with one hand the muslin, and with something concealed in the other. She turned her eyes toward my bedroom to make sure I had gone out.

I imagined she was coming to pay me one of those morning visits, so agreeable to a young husband, and which harmonize so well with the early songs, the first rays, and the pleasant breezes of a summer morning. What other purpose could she have to leave her room so early and in such negligé. I held my breath, and stood motionless as the statues which surrounded me. She passed my door, looking behind with precaution and started toward the reception room, when I intercepted her, asking:

"Ah, my dear, where are you going?"

With a peculiar cry, the cry of a soul which was a hundred thousand leagues from the body, she turned as if moved by a spring, leaned against the wall to save herself from falling, and, white as a sheet, put her hand on her heart. I ran to her.

"Oh, how you frightened me," she said. "Do you know that you might kill me that way?"

Drawing a long quivering breath, she smiled, and pressed my hand for support, and at the same time to let me understand that she forgave me.

"But where were you going?" I repeated.

"Why, to Nounou's room" (the name which Felix had given to his nurse) "to see the baby. Two hours ago, I awoke with a start, I don't know why, quite uneasy about him."

In fact, the nurse's room was at the other end of the apartments.

"And those letters you have in your hand—what about them?"

She looked at them, as though to recall some unimportant matter.

"Oh, I have been writing, because I couldn't sleep; one is to my mother, who was to have come and dined with me in your absence, the other—," she continued; "ah, yes, the other is to a new modiste who has been recommended to me, and I was going to have Nounou deliver them this morning when she takes the baby out. Here are the letters, ask her yourself. I tremble so, see how I tremble. Oh, you must not frighten me so again," and she dropped her head on my shoulder.

I took the letters and, throwing them on the table, returned to my work.

"As a punishment," said Iza, "you must carry me to my room, dearest, I have not the strength to walk. You will have to put me to sleep, for I intended, when I had satisfied my anxiety, and given my orders, to take a nap till noon; I can't do that now unless you help me a little."

I took her in my arms like an infant, and carried her into her room with her face close to mine.

"You don't deserve it," said she, hanging around my neck with a thousand provocations of eyes and lips; "but all the same, you have done well to remain. It is not a good plan for people who love each other so, to be too far apart these beautiful days, and I love you more than ever. Do you know, I would not have liked it if you had left me all alone for three days? And, now, do you love me?"

When I, an hour later, kissed her good-by, she called after me in languid tone: "Don't forget my letters. I don't want anybody to come and disturb us today, not even my mother. If Nounou has gone out, give them to the chamber-maid."

Don't you think, my friend, another might have been deceived, as well as myself? And, but for accident, but for fatality, I would today be ignorant that one of those envelopes contained the most infamous, the most audacious treachery.

How that woman knew me! How sure she was of my confidence, of my blindness, of my stupidity.

I went to the nursery to kiss my little son, my morning custom, and give Nounou the letters.

I had spent a good while in putting Iza to sleep. It was nine o'clock. Nounou was not around. I called the chambermaid. My servant told me that she had just gone down, and could hardly be out of the yard. I opened the window, saw no one, but my dog at the door of the stable. He looked at me, wagging his tail.

It was a splendid day. Not being so much in humor for work as in the early morning, I took my hunting cap and whip, went down-stairs, and proud and smiling, like a man who is sure he is loved, I directed my steps toward the Avenue Marbeuf. I had not gone ten paces when I met the chambermaid returning. "Madame gave me some orders for you," I said, "but you were not around. Should she wake before I come back, tell her that I have attended to them myself." I left the one note at the residence of the countess, and went on to the Rue du Marche d'Aguesseau, No. 12. This was the address of the other letter for Madame Henri, modiste. Why should I not call upon Madame Henri, and pay Iza the compliment of selecting a bonnet to my own taste?

"Madame Henri?" I inquired of the concierge, who, attired in his Sunday suit, was standing in his loge.

"Madame Henri?" he repeated, "no such person here."

"How is that," I replied, "this is No. 12?"

"Yes."

"Rue du Marche d'Aguesseau?"

"Yes; but there is no Madame Henri in this house."

"A modiste," I urged.

"There is no modiste here," replied the man in insolent tones.

"Excuse me," called out his wife, who was finishing her morning duties inside, and without even looking at the questioner. "Yes, there is a Madame Henri in the house, but she is in the country. If you have a letter for her, please leave it."

I had asked for Madame Henri in so natural a manner, and without any special anxiety, that the concierge had not taken the trouble to look me over. After she had spoken she came out, and seeing me in a summer jacket and cap, with a dog, she took me for a messenger of no particular importance.

"Your letter will be forwarded, never fear." At the same time, she gave a little shrug of the shoulders, as much as to say: I know all about it.

Evidently this woman had not thought it worth while to account to her husband for all the private profits of her office.

At this movement of hers, a lightning flash penetrated, not my mind, but my head; I had one of those giddy sensations which usually precede apoplexy. Without distinguishing anything, I saw through all. The concierge extended her hand to take the letter, which I put back in my pocket instinctively. "I will return tomorrow," I said, "when the lady may be here."

"It is not worth while, you have not been told to deliver it to the person herself, have you? You had better leave it."

"No."

"Well, do as you please."

I went away, trembling all over, my feet cold, my head in a vise, my heart standing still. In the street, I leaned against a wall. With an involuntary prayer, which lasted perhaps a second, I entreated God that it might not be true. I broke the seal, and read:

"Impossible for us to see each other. He is not going to the hunt. *Pense à moi*. I kiss thy dear mouth."

No signature. None was needed. I returned to the loge of the concierge. She had resumed her interrupted occupation, and was wiping a cup. I see her now, that abominable creature who for a few pieces of gold aided a man to deceive me, and found it quite natural. Oh, at such a moment, for the power of Nero; to kill with the most horrible torture the wretch who had helped to overwhelm me with anguish, to tear out her entrails, to break her limbs, to hear her howl, curse, pray, and neither to pardon her nor the youngest and most innocent of her children.

Irresistible demand for vengeance; the thirst for blood. Ay, all cruelty, all treachery, all infamy are but the natural and logical right of humanity against the individual who had struck my honor, my love, my soul an irreparable blow. It is possible the evil may often be done in ignorance, but that is not my concern. It is his, to know it.

I returned to the loge, and closed the door behind me. "You will have to tell me everything," I commanded threateningly. The woman hesitated.

"What is there to tell you?"

"To whom is this letter addressed?"

"You can see for yourself."

"Don't mock me, I will strangle you."

I could no longer master myself. The man moved toward me.

"We are respectable people," said he, "and you must leave."

"You are rascals, you are accomplices in crime, and if you don't answer me, I will have you both arrested."

They looked at each other.

"I know very little about it," replied the woman, "but I will tell you what I know; I have done nothing wrong. The first floor apartment is let to a gentleman."

"And his name?"

"M. Henri. He has given me no other name. He pays in advance, and as there is furniture in the apartment for security, I have no need to ask anything further."

"He lives in that apartment."

"No, he comes here from time to time."

"Alone?"

"Yes, alone,"

"For the purpose of meeting a woman?"

"I don't know; he receives whom he chooses, it is none of my business."

"How long has this been going on?"

"For a year, or two years, perhaps."

"Show me the apartment."

"I haven't the key."

"Do you know the real residence of that man?"

"No."

"This letter, then, was for him?"

"Evidently. Now, see here, I don't like this sort of thing. I have a tenant who sees the people he chooses, who calls himself M. Henri, and I hand him the letters that come for Madame Henri. If that is not enough, go to the Police Commissaire, first street to the left. I know what I am about, and I don't care for you."

Muttering, "You are right," I went into the street, staggering like a drunken man. It seemed to me, not that I was becoming insane, but idiotic. I feared I should begin to laugh and sing. I tried to think of things that bore no relation to what had happened. Historical facts, the terms of a book of chemistry which I had read quite recently, came to divert my mind, as in a delirium. Another minute, and I fell with my face to the ground in a stupor. I was afraid of dying there, unrevenged. I rallied my strength and ran toward my house. I recognized, as in a dream, one of our tradesmen, who saluted me. I returned his salute mechanically. My dog, seeing me run, gambolled playfully at my side.

"Who is it? Who is it?" I reiterated in my fever. And the names of all my friends passed before me. As I entered my yard, I stopped. The certainty was too near; I was breathless, I had come so rapidly. Perhaps I should first go to the countess. That letter which I had left at Avenue Marbeuf surely contained some details. Suppose I go there? No. What need had I of details? Those two lines, did they not tell all? I entered. I made myself as calm as possible. I stopped even a moment in the yard, to assure myself that the dog had followed me. I caressed him when he came to me, and in rising I cast a stealthy glance at the curtains of her window. I saw one of them move. The chambermaid had given her my message. Iza doubtess watched for my return in order to judge from my manner whether or not she had anything to fear. She was deceived at the first appearance. Already dressed, she came to meet me, but had only to look at my face to understand. She stopped and turned pale. She had the strength and audacity to ask:

"What is the matter with you?"

"The name of that man?" And I showed her the letter.

"Be calm, I will tell you all. You shall see that I am not quite so guilty as you think."

There was no longer, then, any room for doubt.

She confessed at once that the letter was written to a man. Before she spoke, I still hoped. I would have given my life with a smile to hear Iza utter, in the face of accusation, the involuntary cry of calumniated innocence. Alas! that hope vanished. She took refuge in explanations.

To have conserved himself till twenty-five for a perfect love; to have then given himself in full confidence and freely to a girl of eighteen; to have been the first to reveal to her the passion which he had only known through her; to have melted into that body and that soul, knowing no longer one from the other; to have made of that being at once the centre and circumference of all that he thought, felt, produced; to have said to himself that she would be the sure consolation in all his trials, disappointments, griefs; to have endured for her sake his mother's death; near her, to have nearly forgotten that death; to have believed everything that creature told him; to have made her the confidant of his illusions, his ambitions, and his faults; to have wept freely and without shame before her; to have passed whole nights at her little feet; to have fainted from love in her arms with all the contortions, the extravagances, the foolish things of a passion, which he believed to be shared by her; to have that very morning possessed this creature, more beautiful, more ardent, more unreserved than ever, and then read a letter such as this, and to see the ghastly truth come forth and tremble upon the lips of that woman. Find me a calamity comparable to this. I defy you!

So, another has seen those beauties which I believed known only to me; another has enjoyed this body which I adored, and my lips have dried upon it the kisses of another. These sacred and secret confidences of love, the words which pleasure breaks between the teeth, the sighs, the hesitations, the appeals, the panting, delirious frenzy of passion have all been heard, provoked, gratified, sated by, and with, another, who contemplated her at his ease. She has submitted to his kisses; she has felt in her bosom all his energies; she has forgotten me; she has laughed at me with another. Divine justice, what shall I do to this woman and to that man?

Let us say it to the shame of human nature: jealousy is absolutely physical. We can forgive where we love a thousand adulterous desires, provided they have not been followed by accomplishment; we can pardon her for having idolized some other man than ourselves, provided she has not belonged to him; in short, we will excuse the soul, if the body has not been a participant. Therefore women deny the physical fact, not through shame, nor remorse, nor modesty, but because they know full well that they can retain possession of us only so long as we believe in the innocence of their bodies, and that this is the farthest limit of our magnanimity, as it is the last concession of our pride.

If, notwithstanding the overwhelming proof I held in my hands, Iza should be able to convince me that she had not been in actual possession (O cowardice of love!) of him, whose "dear mouth she kissed upon the paper," I would pardon her, and, who knows, but I might place the fault upon my own shoulders. She perceived this and set to work to convince me, however impossible or difficult the undertaking might be. The psychologist, who could have witnessed without being seen, the struggle which took place between us, would have been more than ever amazed at the resources, the evolution, and audacity of the feminine mind, as well as appalled at the cruelty of a woman, who, having nothing more to lose, seeks to avenge herself for her humiliation and defeat.

She had said: "I am not quite so guilty as you think." I clung still to those ten words.

"Confess the name of that man, before anything else," I demanded.

"Serge."

"He is your lover?"

"No, I assure you."

"He has been your lover?"

"Hear me. . ."

"I'll hear nothing. Yes or no?"

"No."

"Infamous liar. What do you take me for? What else can the expressions mean in this letter?"

"Let me speak. Do you want me to speak?"

I sat down, or rather I let myself drop into a chair, looking her in the face.

"You know very well I was to marry Serge. I was not acquainted with you then, or, at least, I did not know I should love you, and, one day marry you. I wrote you everything at the time, and of my own volition. But for me you never would have known anything about it. My mother had all her thoughts concentrated on that marriage, which would have been a brilliant one. She wanted to compromise Serge, and to force him into the ceremony in spite of his family. She lacked foresight. We were so young, both of us."

"Do you mean to say you were his mistress before becoming my wife?"

"You know very well to the contrary. Is it possible for you to have any doubts on that point? Suspect me now, if you choose, you have the right, and appearances are against me, but don't stain the commencement of our love. I have, perhaps, been imprudent; but then I had nothing whatever to reproach myself."

That was the word, "imprudent"—nothing else. How well women know the elastic words which admit, without explaining. Unhappily, there are moments when passion is more adroit than deceit.

"Leave the past," I said, "and let us come to the present."

She changed her tactics.

"I have nothing to say," she exclaimed. "You will not believe me in regard to the present any more than you do about the past."

"Very well. I am going to kill your lover. I tell you beforehand."

"What do I care? Do you suppose I love him, whom you call my lover? Kill him, if you think best, the poor boy. Yours will be the remorse."

That last answer was a masterful stroke.

"Well, then, why these expressions of love? Why this lascivious kiss?"

"In our country," she answered, "that does not signify anything. Everybody kisses on the mouth."

I heard that, my friend, with both my ears, I heard it.

The weakness which had unmanned me, disappeared in the presence of the guilty one. I felt, rushing from my heart to my brain, steadily and resistlessly as the tide, a determination to know everything, and the requisite strength to enforce it. Iza's artfulness should not cause me to swerve.

Of what avail to discuss? To punish was the only thing to be done. But what punishment could equal the crime? At this moment I recalled the advice of my dying mother, "If, in any serious event, you need a true friend, call on Constantin. You have no better friend than he." All at once I became so calm that Iza was afraid, in the physical sense. She began to have a presentiment of what the wrath of a man might mean. She looked for a mode of escape, or for some one whom she could call upon for help. I rang.

"What are you going to do?" she asked.

The servant appeared.

"Go at once to M. Constantin Ritz, and ask him to come immediately. It is absolutely necessary for me to see him."

When we were alone, she said:

"What has Constantin to do with this matter?"

"You will see."

"I do not want to remain with you two, you will murder me."

And she made a dash for the door. The name of Constantin aroused her fears more than all my rage. I seized her by the arm, I put my hand on her mouth, and said in a resolute voice:

"If you attempt to leave this room or make an outcry, I will crush you under my feet. I have the evidence. I know my rights. Sit down and wait."

At the same time I pushed her upon a divan, where she lay half fainting.

"I want to see my mother," she murmured.

"Pray God that she doesn't come here at present."

"You have raised your hand against a woman," Iza moaned, "against a woman who cannot defend herself. You are a coward."

Her true nature came at last to the surface.

I made no reply. I decided to remain mute.

How strange! All the different emotions which agitated me for the last hour, gave place to such a sentiment of contempt, that it seemed as if what transpired were not my affair, and that I had never had anything in common with that creature, who appeared to have changed, like the beautiful princess in a fairy tale, into a repulsive reptile.

I picked up my chisel absent-mindedly, just to fill in the time until Constantin came. My hands worked mechanically. All at once the facts rushed on my mind like a blast of steam, and I heard these words ring in my ears: "Kill her."

I turned over the question: "What shall I do to this man?" I sought for some abominable, odious, degrading punishment. I would not have him die. That was not enough, on the contrary, I would have him live; but in despair, cursing me every day, suffering mentally and physically, an object of scorn to men, of contempt to women, of horror to himself.

"Do you propose to create a scandal?" said Iza after a few moments' silence.

"There is still time to prevent an irreparable misfortune," she continued. "I did not write to Serge, I simply used his name to divert your suspicions. I am not such a fool to betray myself in a moment of surprise."

A pause. She went on:

"We shall separate, shall we not? After what has happened we can no longer live together. Send for my mother; let me go away with her, and I promise I will tell you the name of my lover."

"My lover." Was it indeed she, who spoke that word? Was it really I to whom she said it? I did not even articulate, but I felt my heart would burst.

"Well, yes, I have a lover, and I am devoted to him, and I have never loved any one else. If you could only know who it is," she taunted.

"Do kill her!" my fury urged.

The door opened. It was none too soon. Constantin appeared. Seeing him, she grew still more pale. What could there be between them?

"I am not at home to any one," I directed my servant. When we were alone I locked the door of the studio, and put the key in my pocket.

"What is going on?" asked Constantin.

"Madame has a lover. Did you know it?"

Constantin remained silent. I handed him Iza's letter.

"I knew it," he confirmed.

"And his name?"

"Yes."

"And that was the reason you did not call here of late?"

He nodded assent.

"I ask your pardon; I suspected you. Madame told me you were too attentive to her."

"Madame was mistaken."

"Why did you keep me in ignorance?"

"Because your mother beseeched me, and I had a regard for your happiness, although I knew it to be illusory. I said to madame what I thought I ought to say."

"What do you advise me to do?"

"You must separate from madame as soon as possible.

"And the lover?"

"That's my affair."

"Yours?"

"Mine!"

All this was spoken in Iza's hearing, who sat motionless, inspecting her nails, as though it was a matter of no concern to her.

"Then," she interposed, rising, and with the utmost indifference, "it is not necessary for me to remain here any longer; can I go?"

"Whenever you choose."

She went to her room, bolting the door.

Constantin pressed my hand and we embraced each other.

"Don't let her go out before I return," he said. "I shall not be away long, and I must have a talk with you. I am going to see Serge."

"Where does he live?"

"Quite near; Rue de Penthièvre. As to yourself, no weakening, no pardon. You are dealing with a monster; I know her."

I remained alone. These events were so unforeseen, so incompatible with either my real or ideal life, the shock so rude, that I felt dazed. There was nothing to do, however, but follow Constantin's advice.

What support in such a terrible ordeal is the presence and courage of a friend! It inspires us with ambition to show ourselves worthy of him and rise superior to circumstance. I stood ready for battle. Too long had I slept in the tranquillity of fame and love. Unable to extract the arrow which had wounded me, I turned it in the wound, ecstatic with my suffering, intoxicated with my misfortune. I realized the luxury of agony, the passion of the martyr, the defiance cast at the executioner. To separate from Iza, to despise, to forget her, to live for my work and my child, seemed the easiest resolve.

Constantin returned.

"Anything new?" he asked.

"Nothing."

Doubtless Iza from her window had seen him approach, for she reappeared a minute later, prettier than ever. Dressed in a robe of *écru foulard* with a short cape, a straw hat trimmed with violets, dainty high-heeled shoes of bronzed leather, and holding in her elegantly gloved hands a little velvet bag containing her jewelry. She had the appearance of a young girl going out for a promenade. How many times I have enjoyed dressing her myself, when she wanted to take a stroll alone, selecting the most becoming costumes, that *tout le monde* might know her beauty.

"I will send today for everything belonging to me," said she, and walked to the door, which she opened and closed behind her with perfect composure.

XVIII

It could not be! I must have dreamed. That my wife, my love, my name, my honor should thus depart. Leave her home, her child, her husband never to see us more, so simply, so quietly. The door closes, and ended forever are our vows, duty, love! All that we had been to each other, now dead and buried. She reclaimed herself, she was free. She would be seen in the street for any one to admire, to follow, to love.

"Where is she going?" I cried, when Iza had departed.

"Let us consider," said Constantin, looking fixedly at me, "there is as yet no public scandal. If you do feel that you cannot live without her, I'll ask her to return and the secret will rest with us three. You will not be the first man who has held his love higher than his honor. But there must be no retaliation, no reproaches, not even regrets. You must thoroughly comprehend what it is that you undertake. Your wife has had five lovers, to my knowledge."

"My God!"

"She is the most vicious person I ever met, even imagined, and I have the greatest possible contempt for women, especially since I knew this one."

I pressed my hands to my head, fearing my reason would forsake me.

"Five lovers!" I repeated. "Five lovers! What did you say? Tell me their names."

"You are not going to fight all of them, are you? Nothing could be more foolish. Everybody around you knew the conduct of your wife. You were the blind man in the game. Twenty times I have been on the point of posting you, but no one meddles with such affairs unless compelled. In this very room I read her a lecture, that would have shamed a courtesan. I threatened her, proof in hand. My friendship for you caused me to act thus. What do you suppose she replied, with utter cynicism? 'If he saw me do it, he would doubt his own eyes.' But why are you unfaithful to him? He is young, fine-looking, distinguished. He makes you comfortable and happy. 'Have I deceived him with you?' she sneered. 'Well then, mind your own business, and permit me to live as I choose, or denounce me if you prefer. Perhaps it will be the best thing you can do.'"

"When was all this?"

"Since Serge returned; he was the first, and he has survived all the others. With her it is no longer a love affair, nor caprice, nor even lust, it's business."

"Go on, finish me."

"Yes, I will finish you, as I should want a friend to finish me, in like circumstances, because we are men, honorable men, and our usefulness, our lives should not be eternally at the mercy of such wretches, either mistress or wife. In short, Countess Dobronowska first married a rich imbecile nobleman, whom she ruined in the twinkling of an eye, and then left to die, besotted, in a *maison de santé*. A Russian general succeeded the count. One day he settled madame with his cane, having surprised her in the arms of his coachman. There's your mother-in-law. Ah, when woman once degrades herself, she descends rapidly, and ends by eating the mud she has walked in. The son-in-law of the countess, whom she always referred to as her 'daughter's husband,' is in fact a very fine man. He married the elder daughter, expressly stipulating that all intimacy with the mother, to whom he gave a round sum, should cease. Of course she squandered the money. He wished to take Iza with him, to save her, although he knew she was Minati's daughter. He was willing to furnish a dowry for Iza, and find her a husband in his own circle. The countess refused, depending on the girl to restore her fortunes. She went to St. Petersburgh after her sojourn in Paris, with the hope of selling her daughter to the prince in succession, but he showed her the door. They struggled with poverty, as best they could, at Warsaw, until Serge, an innocent like yourself, came their way. He would have married the girl, if his family had not adopted strong measures, as they so well know how to in Russia. Was Iza an accomplice of her mother's? I rather think so. What relations did the young people sustain? You ought to know, unsophisticated as you are.

"This good-natured fellow gave her all the money he could raise; he sacrificed his horses, carriages, jewels, even his furniture. He made a solemn promise to return. I can't say what his family did with him, but the countess and Iza were left in the lurch. You know the sequel. You wrote; you were in love. Did the daughter reform? Wearied, ashamed of all these machinations which netted nothing, did she conclude one fine day to marry and become a good wife, abandoning her mother, as her sister had done? It is possible; you see I am charitable. Yes, let us assume she was honest, when she invoked your aid. Women are capable of anything—even of being good. If you had given her no more rope than a shoe string, you would, perhaps, finally have conquered her bad instincts, as you had everything necessary to satisfy her.

"However, blood will tell. With her alone, you might have pulled through, but the mother was too much for your confiding nature. When Serge attained majority, and came in full possession of his estates, he made inquiries for his ex-fiancée, learned of her wedding, reproached the countess' lack of patience, and declared himself still enamored. She at once realized what she had lost, and made up her mind to recover a portion of it, and exact from adultery what she could no longer expect from marriage. She was not the kind of woman to content herself for any period with your remittances, if she saw an opportunity to increase her revenue. It was then she wrote more frequently to Iza in Polish. Before your very eyes, the intrigue was planned, which you discovered this morning. Your poor mother knew about it, and talked to me repeatedly on the subject. It killed her. The countess established herself at Paris, her house serving for the first meetings between her daughter and Serge, until, ashamed of this ignoble complicity, he hired and furnished luxuriously the apartment in Rue de Marché d'Aguesseau. The alleged restitution of a Polish estate was money from Serge. The diamonds and emeralds Iza received from her sister, presents from Serge. The anonymous letter advising you to follow your wife, the invention of the countess. A tombstone procuress. What an idea!

"You ask: 'How did you learn these details?' Through Serge, from whom I found a way to extract them. As to the others, I have them from my brother-in-law, who in turn received them from his colleagues in the Russian embassy. This explains the coolness of my father and sister toward your wife.

"All that has happened is very much your own fault, my poor innocent friend. Continence and chastity are good in their way, but it would have been better for your peace of mind, and your work, if you had, like myself, travelled round a little. You could then have learned to be on your guard against golden locks, sapphire eyes, marble bosoms, and all the physical charms of femininity. You could then have learned that when one is foolish enough to marry, it isn't necessary to add to that folly by marrying an exceptionally beautiful woman.

"Such women were not made for the quiet joys of married life. They are to be painted, to be modelled, to be sung, to be loved—but to be married, never. Dignity, modesty, family duty, goodness, virtue, even love are closed books to them; these belong to ordinary women, each according to her kind. Created for pleasure, these ladies recognize no other law than caprice. Born to inspire, not to endure, they will not brook control, or do anything likely to mar their contour. They look upon marriage as a spring board from which they can leap to intrigue. The husband is of trifling importance provided he is in a position to set off their beauty. The lover is of still less consequence. They do not often consider either the rank, intelligence, or age of the adorer. To shine and to reign—this is their mission. They are like sovereigns, to whom all acclamation is homage. If they have at their feet but a lackey, the worship of that lackey is what they demand. More than one case can be cited where they descended so low.

"The fable of Diana and the shepherd, who was preferred to the gods, symbolizes this. Thus we have the brazen indecencies, the scandalous amours of celebrated historical beauties. These anomalies are logical. Beauty, like all royalty, admits only inferiors, therefore, to a remarkably beautiful woman, a remarkably handsome man is neither an admirer nor a lover, he is an equal, that is to say, an enemy. If she surrenders herself to him, she does not give, she exchanges. A celebrated man is not in her line, for she will only enter into his glory as an accessory. She has a husband, honored, distinguished. Society follows him, flatters him, and leaves him hardly a moment to himself. His wife will easily find an hour to spend in a furnished room, almost a garret, where awaits an obscure lover, ill looking and perhaps old, but whom she thrills and dazzles, who prostrates himself before her with an admiration amounting almost to ecstasy, to frenzy. To her own husband she is only beautiful; to that man she is a goddess, and for that she has come.

"In a delicious, studied pose, which magnifies her charms, smiling, unveiled, she gives herself to that fascinated mortal, and watches with eager eyes to see how he loves her, comparing the expression of this one with the other, for she is refined, this woman; her mind and her senses seek for novelty, contrasts. That night she will offer the same spectacle to her husband, tomorrow to some other lover. Some day, without telling them why, because they no longer amuse her, she will see these men no more, and if they suffer, if they die, so much the better. She will watch how they suffer, after she has watched how they loved.

"She is like unto those pale and silent divinities of India, who require a sacrifice of blood. While their worshippers cast palpitating human flesh at their feet, they look tranquilly upon the horizon with eyes of precious gems.

"Such a woman," continued Constantin, "is she whom you have married, my poor fellow. You have innocently developed her natural sensuality; you have foolishly presented the mysteries of her beauty to the eyes of the profane. You have immortalized her, and lost her a little sooner by so doing. Your admiration did not suffice. After passing from hand to hand, embodied in marble and bronze, she could not resist the desire to reveal herself to believers and sceptics alike.

"A venal Galatea, she became animate for the first comer, and not content with offerings of flowers, of love, of tears and blood, she craved diamonds and gold. Every one knew of her conduct. Those who did not make you an accomplice, held you at any rate responsible. The world won't believe that a man of your fibre could be so hoodwinked without knowledge or profit. When they learn of your grief, they will say, it is well played. Your subsequent life proves you have been only unfortunate.

"As to the names of these men; what is the use? They owe you nothing, and they despise your wife as much as you do. You are the victim of an accomplished act. The identity of the actors is of no moment.

"Do you know why she went away so calmly just now? Because she promptly saw her advantages in the situation. She paid you the compliment to justify herself a little. The intuitive thought of a guilty woman is to deny, but she has no need of your forgiveness. It is on Serge's account that you send her away, it is to Serge she goes, and Serge is rolling in wealth. Do you see? It is dishonor, it is prostitution, but it is luxury, and the moderate comfort with which you surrounded her was too humble an environment for her taste. She dreamed of the celebrity of Aspasia, of Marion Delorme, and of Ninon. But that is wherein she will be punished. And it is I, who have found her punishment.

"Instead of challenging Serge, endangering your life and his, I have told him what has occurred, and informed him, as I have you, what kind of a woman she is. I have pledged my word that there shall be no further hostilities, if he would swear never to see Iza again, nor assist her financially, convincing him how ridiculous it would be to risk his life for such a creature, and how great his remorse should he kill you. He has sworn, and he is a man of his word. Honor has its degrees, its shadings. A man may steal the wife of another, whether he knows him or not, drive him to desperation even, and yet be incapable of defrauding him of a single sou, or of violating his word in the slightest particular. I did not make humanity, I take it as I find it. Your adorable little wife is therefore to be reduced to living with her mother, from whom Serge, likewise, will cut off supplies. Their ill-gotten diamonds will soon be swallowed, and they themselves will revert unto poverty, which is the shame, the despair, and the punishment of courtesans. Amen."

"And I?"

"As for yourself, let my sister bring up your child with her own, till he is of an age to be a consolation to you, and you must depart for Florence or Rome and seek solace in grand art, and I will go along to keep you from blowing out your brains at some corner. When you need a woman do as I do, pay her what she is worth, which will not be a ruinous sum. When you are cured, for you will be cured, come and live among those who truly love you. Is it agreed?"

"It shall be as you say."

"Then sleep this evening at my house. You will find the night long, but I shall be there. Tomorrow, we start upon our journey. Rome, Florence, and Venice, there is nothing more beautiful in the month of September. And now, let us try to think no more of your troubles. We will pack our trunks."

XIX

All of us have, some philosopher hath said, strength sufficient to bear the misfortunes of others.

To this strength, and perhaps to the secret pleasure of giving consolation, Constantin owed the animation and good humor with which he delivered, at such length, his satire on the beauty and character of Iza. True in every point, but a truth which burned my wound like a red-hot iron. This cauterization was evidently the best remedy for me, and, had I been in the place of my old friend, I should have probably applied it the same as he; but I leave you to imagine how I enjoyed the ordeal. By sheer will power, I refrained from crying aloud, expecting to fall dead at any moment. Ah, what cannot the brain of man endure!

I was married under the system of the separation of property. My lawyer with foresight had held to that clause. It would be, he said, an advantage even to my wife, to whom it assured the disposition of that marvellous fortune, which was always on the point of coming. Besides, I could appoint Iza, if I should choose, my general legatee. In reality, he had sought to avoid that, through joint possession, I should ever be at the mercy of this foreign girl, who did not inspire his practical mind with much confidence. I had not therefore to render any account to Iza, inasmuch as she had brought no values into the partnership. I ordered the furniture in her room appraised, for I could not permit it to go with her into her new life. The sum fixed by the expert I remitted to Constantin, to be included with the things she was to send for. Each of these objects was a memento and a grief.

I paid and dismissed the servants, all of whom had aided my wife to deceive me, from Nounou to the chambermaid. Fatal and inevitable solidarity between the base in sentiment and the low in position. I made no allusion to their complicity. I stated, as a pretext for dismissal, the necessity of an immediate departure, and I even made them some little presents. I sent away the child with his little personal property and his favorite playthings to Madame de Niederfield; and solitude enveloped me. The day was nearly ended. Darkness, little by little, gathered upon the walls of these rooms, where I had been so happy but a few hours before.

Constantin, with a cigar in his mouth, arranged the papers, quiet at home, asking from time to time, "Shall I burn this? Shall I save that?" and putting the keys in his pocket, as one by one he emptied the drawers. The bell rang. Had Iza returned? Had she something to say? I went to open the door—it was the porters asking for the baggage of a lady, who was waiting at a house in Avenue Marbeuf. I showed them what to take, and watched the boxes carried out as if each were the body of a friend. When the men had gone for the last time, the clock struck eight.

"Let us be off," said Constantin, "we have nothing more to do here. I will send for your trunks."

I made no reply and followed him. Descending the stairs, my head reeled and I was obliged to catch hold of the rail.

We entered a restaurant. My companion made me eat what he chose, and eat heartily to dull my memory and distract my thoughts, but I declined to drink. I knew the effect of stimulants on my temperament. Besides, wine brings no consolation, it only numbs a sorrow, which reappears later, keener and more poignant.

The repast finished, Constantin took me to his house, crossing the Boulevards. I looked at the passing crowd as though I had no longer anything in common with the rest of humanity. It seemed, a shadow myself, I dwelt in the land of shadows. Now and then my mother's name struck my heart.

Constantin gave me his bed, taking himself the sofa. I did not lie down, however. I walked from one room to another. Seeing that I could not sleep, he suggested:

"Suppose you go to see my father."

"No, not this evening; tomorrow."

He began to write.

The noises of the street gradually died away, only the ticking of the clock was heard, tick by tick it counted my life, for which I had no further use. I cannot say that I suffered. My brain, which, every evening at this hour rested from the fatigues of the day, seemed to say: "First recover your strength, tomorrow we will hold counsel."

I stretched myself on a divan, lighted a cigar, and fixed my attention upon a certain point on the wall. Finally I fell into a sort of stupor.

I remained thus until five o'clock in the morning, when I opened my eyes confidently, like one waking from restful sleep; but my grief awoke also. It enlarged, approached me, seated itself at my pillow. A sudden sting made my heart leap in my breast. I remembered the cause, I found myself on my feet, not knowing why.

Immediately the terrible events of the previous day began to revolve about me like savages around a prisoner at the stake. I called to my aid Constantin's arguments, the resolutions with which he had inspired me. They were hot enough to withstand the furies whose cries became more and more threatening.

"How is it," they howled in my ears, "how is it, there is a man who has taken your honor, your happiness, your future, and you let him remain in peace; you content yourself with his promise which he will perhaps break? The punishment inflicted upon your wife is but a cowardly act. Does it satisfy you? Would Constantin, had he been in your shoes, have acted thus? Supposing you had taken his sister, would he, a soldier, not have killed you? Above everything, blood!"

Bah! I was a fool yesterday.

And without a thought as to the early hour, I ran to Rue Penthièvre, and presented myself at Serge's house. The valet did not wish to rouse his master; I insisted, explaining that it was a family matter of grave importance. I had come expressly from abroad. The valet ushered me into a boudoir hung in blue satin.

The first object that met my eyes was the terracotta bust I had made of Iza, at fifteen, and which she had told me was in the possession of her sister. I seized an andiron from the fire-place and broke it in a thousand pieces.

Serge appeared, and saw this strange spectacle. He doubtless knew me; he comprehended, and waited on the threshold. Perhaps he feared that I would assassinate him with a blow of the andiron, which I still held in my hand.

Serge was a large young man, with a frank and open countenance, neither handsome nor ugly, every inch a lord.

In a hollow voice I announced my name.

"You are not suited then, sir, with what was agreed upon between your friend and myself," he replied, in the tone of a man about to lose his patience. "That is no reason for breaking an article which does not belong to you."

"That bust?" I cried.

"That bust is my property; I paid for it, and I am in my own house. Please state the object of your visit."

"I want to kill you, sir."

"You should have said so at once, it would have been much more simple. If you are as anxious as I, meet me at eleven o'clock with your

ALEXANDRE DUMAS, FILS

witnesses, in the forest of St. Germain at the gate of the terrace. Name whatever weapon you choose."

He rang. The valet appeared, I took my hat.

"Pick up the pieces of that bust," Serge ordered, "and throw them away."

Then, having saluted me, he returned to his chamber.

XX

I had placed myself in a false and ridiculous position; but I had, at least, given vent to my turmoil of passion. I knew now how to employ this first day, which otherwise would have seemed interminable.

I found Constantin up and looking all over for me.

I informed him of the situation.

"It is foolishness," he said; "but I should have done the same. Go and see my father and kiss your son, while I summon one of my comrades."

At the hour mentioned we were at the rendezvous. I had chosen the sword, being passably expert with this weapon; Serge drew better than I, and merely defended himself. Realizing this, the blood flushed my cheeks, and with my left arm bent across my forehead, holding the sword in my right like a lance, I ran recklessly upon my adversary, who, not foreseeing the blow, could not parry it. He fell. I had pierced his right side.

"The stroke is not according to rule," he said, "but it counts all the same. If I die of it, monsieur, I want you to know that I should have been in despair had I caused you any pain: if I recover, let me reassure you of my promise; there shall exist no relations of any kind between myself and the person in regard to whom we have met. Besides she is already notified to that effect."

The wounded man was taken to the Chateau du Val, and we returned to Paris.

"A good task accomplished," said Constantin, as he kissed me when we were alone. "It has relieved you a little."

"Yes, indeed."

"That is excellent. Let us hope Serge will recover. He is a brave man. You are the victim, he the dupe. You have nothing to reproach yourself with, and my plan stands good. What a face Iza will make when she learns of his determination. Honestly, she ought to have been contented with a husband such as you, and a lover such as he. There are none better."

On returning to Constantin's house I found a messenger who handed me this letter:

"Situated as we are now, there is no longer reason to conceal anything. You need not keep Felix in your charge. He is not your child. Give me authority to take him from where he is, and you will hear no more of him nor his mother.

Izabella Clemenceau,
née Dobronowska

I passed the letter to Constantin.

"She lies," he said, "you know it as well as I do. Her little scheme will not work; she wants to be revenged on you. She is perfect. 'Née Dobronowska' is a master stroke. One has the whole woman in those two words. There is nothing to do but laugh at it."

Then, addressing the messenger, and handing him a five-franc piece:

"Tell that lady it is all right; we keep the child; say we are going away, and that your fee is paid. And now," he added, turning to me, "rest easy, Felix will not leave my sister's, and your wife shall not enter there. En route."

Constantin was correct. That ebullition of passion, that rage and bloodshed, had relieved me. I should have felt the same alleviation in seeing my own blood flow. I needed something heroic, to get outside of me everything fomenting within. If I had not challenged Serge, I should have challenged some one, I don't know whom, at the first opportunity. Nature, in such matters, is wiser than all reasoning and all philosophy. She demands that we shall throw ourselves, recklessly, upon our enemy. Kill or be killed, but whatever happens, we are assuaged.

In fine, I satisfied myself. I could meet M. Ritz, his daughter, and his son-in-law with much less embarrassment than on the previous evening. I had taken the broad way to save my honor. I could not be accused of weakness. I might be pitied, but not despised. I might be unhappy, but I was no longer a subject of ridicule. As to Serge, I bore him no ill-will, and his conduct on the field compelled me to esteem him. I need not explain all these sentiments. You are a man, you understand them. In short, Iza appeared to have been violently and forever expunged from my life. It even seemed to me I ought to remain at Paris, the projected journey was unnecessary, and I could meet that woman with impunity. What had happened to me, had been the fate of many another.

There remained to me health, occupation, fame, good conscience, the esteem and friendship of honest people, all these things of which one alone, in my ambitious days, I should have deemed sufficient for the happiness of my whole life. Thank God it is not in the power of one woman to overturn the world by her faults! The sun, the spring time, the flowers, art, youth, beauty, even love still exist. If this woman had not lived I could have done very well without her. Perhaps my talent needed a violent shock to become genius. What would Michael Angelo have done in my place? He would have shrugged his shoulders, and made a master-piece. Without going so far, how would the most obscure of men have sought distraction in a similar case?

Work and forget.

"Why should I trouble Constantin?" I said to M. Ritz. "Why disarrange his habits? I am strong, I assure you; and in good spirits. I am roused from a dream, that is all. I have been in love with a beautiful girl; that would come to me sooner or later. I have possessed her, and she is dear to me, and I do not regret her. I will take up my life again as if nothing had happened; I will see a little more of you. Am I no longer a part of your family? Your daughter will bring up my son with her own children. I shall even work better now, having more freedom." The worthy man heard me with attention; he looked upon me with tenderness, as an experienced physician when an invalid seeks to persuade that he is cured, and who pretends to believe it in order to tranquillize him, before there is a new crisis.

"You are quite correct," he said; "but the journey seems to me none the less necessary. After every fall, we should walk a little to be sure that nothing is broken. Go to Rome; it will be useful in many ways. If I were not old and tired, I would accompany you; the youth and vivacity of my son will make him a more agreeable companion; and, besides, I do not need going to Rome to convince me that I am no longer good for anything."

XXI

We passed through Switzerland, Lombardy, Tuscany; we visited Venice, Milan, Boulogne, Pisa, Florence. Constantin was delighted with me. He had never travelled so profitably. I explained to him the architecture of the different schools, as exemplified in the public buildings. It was a constant surprise to him to see my mind so clear and, at times, jovial.

He grew more familiar with my idiosyncrasies. I analyzed my sentiments. How well we think we know ourselves!

The nearer I approached Rome, the keener became the desire to reach there, and my ambition for work grew apace. I was well equipped. Perseverance and practice added to the gifts of nature. I had a right to consider myself one of the first artists living in France; but so incomparably inferior in all respects to those great masters Italy would shortly reveal to me.

There, in their natural soil, they had sprung forth and produced a galaxy of marvellous expressions, any of which, in our time, would have immortalized its author. My brain, tense from recent emotions, needed a plunge into the cool waters of reflection.

We reached our destination about the middle of October. You do not know the Eternal City. It is useless to describe it. The day was ending, shadows lengthened, the wind swayed the trees, clouds dashed against each other. The dust whirled, the thunder growled, streaks of lightning rent the threatening horizon. The storm came. I had no longer time to gaze upon the roadway. However, I can say that Rome at once appeared to me the natural refuge of the unhappy; if the remembrance and evidence of the most notable catastrophe can console or strengthen him who suffers under an individual grief. Scarcely do you enter Rome, when you are impressed, overshadowed, surrounded by the imposing lessons of philosophy, taught by these ruins.

You have seen Versailles. The grand siècle, in passing away, has left upon the royal residence, the deserted gardens, its abandoned palaces, its streets, its silent divinities, and impassive waters, even over its future inhabitants, a sort of half-tone which the sun will never again pierce. You walk, so to speak, upon tip-toe, fearing to waken some one. Well, Versailles is Rome with a difference. There are twenty centuries between the throne and the cross, between the grand and the immense, between the man and the God. Versailles is the mummy of an epoch; Rome is the skeleton of a world.

After forty-eight hours in the ancient city, I felt that I was saved. The man was absorbed in the artist. In the presence of all these splendors my private sorrow appeared small and mean. My eyes, astonished, dazzled, could not take in the imposing lines of vast spaces. It vanished. It would be unheard of audacity, insensate conceit to presume to suffer in the shadow of that Coliseum where so many thousands of men, women, and children, enduring the most awful tortures, had died smiling.

I wrote to M. Ritz thanking him for his excellent advice, and telling him of my mental serenity. I invited him to come and join me; for as the gentle lad of twenty returned to me, resolute and whole-hearted, I prepared to recommence my life.

Constantin and I walked about the city from morning till eve. He accompanied me everywhere, took an interest in everything, only insisting that from five to six o'clock I would consent to promenade at the Pincio, or at the Villa Borghese, the rendezvous of the Roman ladies and distinguished invalids who come, during the winter, to seek in that climate a few years' reprieve. He planned his father's settlement near me, with his daughter and son-in-law. M. de Niederfield would have to change his embassy, a change which could be readily effected. Constantin would arrange all when he reached Paris.

Intelligent people appreciated my work; glory would compensate me for love. So much the worse for that woman who had neither seen nor appreciated my worth, and who could so ignore as to betray me. She was dead to me, dead indeed.

Did my new friends know the real cause of my leaving Paris? Was their sympathy increased by the need I had of being sustained, and strengthened? I believe so; for none spoke of my wife, though all knew me to be a married man. Were they acquainted with the affair through their Paris correspondents, or the indiscretion of Constantin? It makes little difference. They knew of it, and not yet having attained to the age of pitiless rivalry, of mortal strife, they did not forge my sorrow into a weapon against me; on the contrary, by the most delicate attention they sought to divert my thoughts.

Alas! The hand of destiny. Notwithstanding all our efforts I was not to escape. Constantin, being recalled to duty, left Rome, promising faithfully that he would return in a month, with or without his family. The guardianship he exercised had grown quite onerous, and I began making preparations for numerous works, which his presence, it seemed to me, had retarded. I accompanied him to Civita Vecchia. We embraced as though we were separating for eternity, rather than as friends who meet again in a few days; and when the boat which bore him disappeared in the distance, I returned to Rome, crossing the green Campagna with its gentle undulations, its scattered pine groves, the home of wild bulls, thick set and vigorous, lying motionless under the great trees, resembling at a distance boulders fallen from the neighboring mountains.

XXII

Impatient to resume that life so rudely interrupted, I arranged my tools, prepared my clay, and rolled up my sleeves, as in those days when the morning inspiration made me leap joyfully from the bed in which love had put me to sleep. Alas! The power of work is not a slave, to obey at the first call; Inspiration is not a courtesan, whose smile is always ready.

A man who devotes his life to a mechanical occupation, or even to one of those liberal arts which serve and live by the necessities of others, such as Medicine or Law, let such a man seek consolation in his employment, the answer will come immediately; distraction will be forced upon him. Strangers knock at his door, morning, noon, evening, and night. His attention, knowledge, presence, are called upon. His mind will no longer have a single moment for self-communion. Importuned, fatigued, besieged; willing or unwilling, he is impelled into the busy whirl, and habit finally dissipates his sorrow.

The lines, the gestures, the attitudes, the action which I found so readily in the impatient enthusiasm of youth, in the genial joys of love, were now rebellious and difficult to catch. My eye saw not, my hand had lost its cunning. I looked at my rough-hewn clay, but the ideas came not, and I remained whole days motionless before it, then I stumbled for the first time upon these words: "To what end?" Mystic agents of destiny who attend, at a certain moment, every man who demands from life more than it contains, and flings him bruised and despairing back upon his track. In short, the heart had nullified the brain, and through the excesses of sensation I had arrived at mental impotence. The young men who were interested in my work, endeavored in vain to incite me to action.

"Master," they said, "what are you going to do for us? We are waiting to see you at your work."

I explained to them that I was not yet ready. It was necessary to conceive well in order to execute well. I developed to them my theories of art; I launched into the aesthetic. I confessed myself intoxicated by the wonders before my eyes; I asked permission to first recover my breath; as much as possible I concealed the truth. Then in turn, I went to see them. I listened as they timidly confided their projects; I examined the rough-casts they submitted with emotion, for they

ALEXANDRE DUMAS, FILS

recalled my youth, still so near, already so far. Their essays were incorrect, but they had faith. They believed in the future. To them, life was only embarrassed by material difficulties. I had known poverty. I explained how easily it could be traversed, the will aiding. Further, I was ready with assistance if they wished, and I opened my purse, which they closed without drawing from it. Then I gave them advice, not only in the way of art, but for their private lives as well. Without offering myself in illustration, I endeavored to warn them against love, which is, I assured them, the great danger for the artist. My heart, for three months too full, had needed an outlet. I instinctively sought sensations differing from my personal emotions, wherein I might find relief.

One day I surprised in myself a base and vile sentiment, which I had never before encountered. One of these young men uncovered a figure he had just finished, a masterpiece of taste, grace, action, and proportion. You doubtless know it as well as I; it is *La Fille aux Grappes*, which brought to its author the Prix de Rome; and at the last exposition of sculpture was a unanimous and united success.

Do you know what was my first feeling on seeing that figure? A sentiment of envy, let me be frank, of hate against him who had executed it. A little more and I should have seized a hammer and destroyed that marble. So quick to evil is this being which I carry within me. A cloud passed over my eyes. I had the strength to restrain myself; I extended to the unsuspecting young man a hand moist with perspiration. "It is one of the most beautiful things I have ever seen, even at Rome," I said to him, "and I predict for you a great triumph."

For several days I thought of nothing but that Bacchante. If I had seen it at the time when I could work, I should have embraced its author, for then it would have seemed to me that I had nothing to fear from him; but now, unhappy, exiled, condemned to inaction and sterility, I beheld in this confrère, a rival and an enemy. It is not easy to be impartial and benevolent when one loses something by it, and from that moment I appreciated much more all that Thomas Ritz had done for me.

I had begun to calm myself a little when a comrade of the young sculptor informed me that he had obtained his statue from a Greek cameo, found at Pompeii. It was a copy, a plagiarism, a theft. He never could get beyond it, he was a quack, not a genius. I forgave him. Such, my friend, is man, even a man of talent. How disgraceful. And now, I asked myself, why not imitate this young man, why not, in my turn, borrow from the imagination of others? The habitude of success is not easily lost, and no one can know without having experienced it, the tortures of a mind which finds itself declining, and seeks some method of concealment from the world, that it may be valued always as in the past. I was willing to betray the confidence of my young companions. As my imagination would no longer respond to my call, I interrogated theirs, believing it to be fruitful because it was young, with the secret intention of appropriating their ideas.

I wandered through the museums, the private galleries; I examined cameos, medals. I had never been able to draw inspiration from others. I was still less able to do it now. I began upon ten different subjects, I did not finish one, my thoughts were absent.

That miserable woman had stolen my soul and my genius.

XXIII

C onstantin did not return.

In the first communication I received from him he expressed an intention to do so, but the wheel of Parisian life had drawn him into its cogs.

M. Ritz, in writing to his son during our journey, had avoided any allusion to Iza. On his return to Paris, Constantin with his usual frankness gave me all the particulars concerning her, the more so, as he believed my wound entirely healed—a supposition which I had not cared to disturb.

When Iza learned of my departure, she was furious, and preferred a complaint against M. Ritz, whom she accused of illegally detaining her son. She endeavored to interest M. Dax, a former admirer, in the suit. He not only declined the honor, but instructed the judge as to the previous conduct of the plaintiff.

She then tried the effect of her charms upon the jurors; they were impregnable, and M. Ritz was authorized to retain the custody of Felix, whom his mother, however, might see once a week, in the presence of some member of the family. For a little while Iza came regularly; then but once in two weeks, and finally ceased altogether.

She was living plainly with her mother, dressed like a young girl, and did not appear to be more than eighteen. She never before seemed so modest and respectable. Among strangers she was called mademoiselle. Constantin caused her to be tracked and watched, but nothing detrimental was discovered. As additional surety, Serge, on his recovery, left Paris. Constantin saw him several times, and they conversed freely. Serge was very fond of Iza; and desiring to keep his promise to me, he judged it more prudent to go away. Nevertheless, she could not as yet be without resources. Before the duel he had given her several large sums, besides other presents; eighty or a hundred thousand francs, which she had invested judiciously. Extravagant passion and good business judgment is not uncommon with women.

Our separation made a great sensation. I so famous, she so beautiful. The truth was well known, notwithstanding the statements of the countess and her daughter. All respectable families closed their doors to them. No society remained to the precious pair, but that of men. Men have almost always something to gain from these conjugal catastrophes, hence they take the part of, and interest themselves in the woman so long as she is pretty, or until they themselves are married, whereupon they affect to ignore her. Some cause had to be assigned for our quarrel, of a nature to make it appear my fault. Therefore I had deserted the domestic fireside, they said, and gone off to Italy with my mistress, first using up my wife's dowry, and even keeping her trousseau, which I gave to "the other one." If I had not gone away, she would have left me. Now she could tell everything: I had compelled her to serve me as a model, and wanted a cast made of her by my assistants; she refused so firmly that I did the work myself. I had exposed the moulds to all comers, and brought rich people to my house in order to add to my art a secret and profitable industry. La Buveuse was the exact reproduction of her, etc., etc., etc.

Such was the tenor of Constantin's letters. There is no need to tell you any more about it, you see from this the procession of calumnies and retaliations. The stories were listened to, people believed them or not, and passed on to other things. Paris has not much time to give to any one individual.

But the fact of the duel, and M. Ritz's affirmation, held public opinion in my favor.

XXIV

H ere is some news for you," wrote Constantin later on. "Your wife and her mother have disappeared, after having sold their movables. It seems they do not intend to favor Paris with their presence again. *Bon voyage!* I am glad for your sake. There is nothing now to prevent your return, for you are not going to remain forever in the Eternal City. They are supposed to be in England, or Holland or Germany or Sweden. At any rate, they have not gone to join Serge. I have received word from him. He is at St. Petersburgh, and intends to marry."

At these tidings about the departure of Iza, can you guess what passed through my mind? I imagined she had repented; that she conducted herself with so much propriety since my departure for the purpose of convincing me of her repentance; that she still loved me; that she had gone away without saying anything to any one in order to rejoin me; that I should behold her at my door, imploring pardon, vowing she could not live without me, and satisfactorily explaining the horrid past as the result of physical folly, of an aberration in which her will had no part.

Oh, the baseness of the human heart.

XXV

U nder pretext of a ramble in the country, I betook myself to Civita Vecchia, in the belief that Iza would arrive by the next steamer. For eight days, I never left the shore, searching the horizon with a feverish impatience of mind and body, for my senses began all at once to remember and to crave.

Sometimes, when a steamer was signalled, I would take a boat that I might the sooner see her, whom I awaited. I said to myself: "If she returns freely and willingly to seek me, from the love she bears me, I will forget; we will be re-united from this day and the past shall be dead. Let her come within the reach of my hand, and I will take her back. Let the world say what it chooses. What is the world to us? Are we not rather two beings apart from it, each born with his faults, and should we not therefore love each other in a different manner from other mortals? Will I be the first weak man to forgive a weakness? Is not all humanity of the same frail stuff? Are not all the legends of love like unto this? The woman falls, the man suffers; the woman repents, the man pardons. The one thing is to love, to feel ourselves alive, and to give life to other beings, fictitious or real. Love, whatever it may be, is the first element of art; its vital atmosphere. Behold I am unable to create anything, absent from the one I love. She comes! I feel her! I see her!

She did not come.

I saw descending, landing, passing before me, only strangers, unknown, indifferent.

"Perhaps she travelled by land," I consoled myself, and went back to Rome.

I found nothing there.

Only a letter from Madame Lespéron, who had just heard of my troubles. She pitied me, she was glad that I sought to strengthen myself at the sources of Christian poetry, which called to me: "courage! courage!" With French fervor she concluded, "oh, for wings, for wings, who will give me wings?"

I soon perceived that my energies were quite exhausted. The different emotions of surprise, jealousy, rage, revenge, friendship, envy, even forgiveness, had worn me out. I asked only that I might somewhere throw off the burden with which Fate had overloaded my heart and brain.

You have doubtless seen a noble animal, suddenly surprised in the peaceful forest home by the hunter's bullet; it bounds over the bushes and takes refuge in the wood. "I hit him," says the sportsman; but the animal continues its rapid course, pursued by the cries of the hounds; little by little they tire and lose the scent. If you could follow, you would see it stop and turn its head toward a certain portion of its body, where a few drops of blood begin to trickle. With the persevering instinct of self-preservation, the poor beast runs a little farther, then its legs tremble, it looks about with staring, anxious gaze. Seeing no pursuers, it drags itself to a thicket impenetrable to dogs, to hunters, to all those who cause suffering for mere pleasure, there to die in silent misery.

Like the stricken animal, that which I had taken for strength in the first half of the struggle, was but fever. I was touched in a vital part. Nothing remained for me but to die, and as easily as possible.

I closed my door to the living and happy, to that humanity with which I had nothing now in common. I denied myself to all the young men, who gradually discontinued their visits. I could no longer hope to derive from youth its buoyancy and courage. I passed whole days in the same position, motionless and silent, absorbed in thought.

XXVI

Where could she be? Why had she gone away from France? To what clime had she taken her life and mine? So long as she breathed the same atmosphere that we had breathed together, she still belonged to me. I could see her going and coming in the places so familiar to me. I had been too lenient. I should have caused her arrest; avenged myself. Doubtless she expected I would return. She knew so well how I loved her; she must know I could not live without her. Had she a lover? Another one?

I did wrong to follow the advice of Constantin. He cared little for me.

Should I return to Paris? And, if so, to what purpose? Bring up my child? Bah! his toys are sufficient for him. Besides, do I love him, this child, who is the very image of his mother? Why wait for death? Why not anticipate it? They say suicide is a crime; it is not true. It is the most inalienable right of man, when he suffers beyond endurance. If it be a crime, so much the worse for the God who has forced us to commit it.

Does there exist such a God, whose ministers, exempt from the duties, the trials, and the passions of humanity, prescribe for us, from the depths of their indifference, suffering, strife, and abnegation? What has he done for me, this God, whom they set up before me? The few joyful hours that I have known, did I not pay for them, in advance, by combats with misery, prejudice, injustice, and labor? Have I not again paid for them with tortures of heart, of soul, of spirit? When with tears and supplications I asked this God to leave me my mother, did he accord to me one moment's grace? When, in silent prayer, I beseeched that Iza might not have been untrue to me, did he give me any proof of his power or his goodness? What advice, what help, what consolation have I received from this Master, who for thousands of years has witnessed, unmoved and deaf, the crimes of some, the anguish of others, the everlasting triumphs of evil?

Will humanity never get away from the blind submission to the traditions, the legends, the dogmas which the logic of an infant, with a single word, can destroy? He has had his time, this angry God, of punishing forever and ever, myriads of creatures for the fault of one, who emanated directly from him. If such a God exists, let all humanity deny him, and drive him from its thought and heart; let it leave him alone, in the mystery with which he has enveloped himself, and unshackled march on to the conquest of its rights and its liberty. If mankind needs a God, let it invent one who will be intelligible, and who will make common cause with it. Meanwhile, life is a misfortune, and death a right.

XXVII

As with all who suffer, I made my grief the hub of the universe, toward which everything converged, and I took exception to human and divine laws. Nothing less than the reconstruction of the world would restore to me the place I had lost. All that had been said and done by great souls for the happiness and consolation of men, seemed to me incomplete, false, and unjust.

I passed in review the most shocking and lamentable catastrophes in history. I could have borne them all heroically. But the one which had struck me, seemed beyond my strength.

This is not unprecedented. Certain great disasters, putting their victims above other men, have made of them an everlasting subject of wonder and admiration for each new generation; but these miserable, private misfortunes, ignoble and unpoetic, the recital of which provokes laughter; which human gayety has sung in every key and tongue, and of which one dies slowly and in obscurity, such calamities demand a horizon unobscured and undimmed.

Such were the thoughts and reflections I harbored from morn till eve, and yet they were the least dolorous. During the night I slept but little, and in my insomnia the same pictures invariably presented themselves. I had them perpetually in sight, like the black points that intercept the visual ray, and which the eye mechanically follows through space till, vanishing at the right, they are immediately reproduced at the left.

These tableaux were either grotesque or lascivious, but always abominably real.

I saw Iza sometimes with one, sometimes with another, in different attitudes and postures of passion. I had only to remember, alas, to divine all that I did not see. Then, trembling from head to foot, drenched with a cold perspiration, I would leap from my bed, ready to break everything about me to frighten and chase away this hallucination.

How often in the night have I opened my window with the intention of throwing myself out. How frequently have I uncovered my breast, and standing before the glass felt for the spot where I should strike. At such moments the artist reappeared, through habit, in the midst of my distraction; I sought an attitude for dying. Then the death which I was about to inflict upon myself, seemed insufficient; it was not painful enough for my excited condition. I craved a punishment. I wished to see my bones broken, to hear them crack upon the wheel, that I might find joy in extreme pain, as I had found pain in extreme joy.

But I did not kill myself. I had only the malady, the mania of suicide; an incomprehensible state for whosoever has not passed through it, where one lives, if it may be called living, between the desire and the dread of annihilation. You wish to leave by violence this world where you suffocate, but stop always at the threshold of the next. It is not the secret hope of consolation, nor yet the instinctive fear of suffering, which prevents you, it is the very impossibility of dying. You are under the domination of a vital activity which has no limit and knows no exhaustion. You desire death without a spasm, with exasperation, with frenzy; one hand pushes you on, the other holds you back. You neither live nor die. It is the hysteria of the unknown!

Who would believe a woman's misconduct could cause such perturbations in the brain of man? Ah, I assure you, I have suffered. During my rare moments of lucidity I very well understood that all this trouble came from inaction of a mind accustomed for long years to work, to study, to production, and, for the past few months, compelled to turn over and over continually the same thoughts. I sought food for this famished mind. Do you know what I found? The most insane ideas suggested themselves as the only possible resource: to conspire, to burn, to violate! To be Brutus, Erostratus, or Tarquin. To use for some great crime the disgust which I had for life, and, since I could not immortalize myself by noble works, to become immortal through some odious deed. When you see a man stricken with an overpowering sorrow hide and bury himself in utter solitude, you may be sure he is upon the road to madness. It is but a question of time.

XXVIII

H owever, I must choose; either to live or die.

One evening—it was nearly three months since I had seen a human being, except my valet—I made an effort; I determined to tear myself out of this solitude and launch abruptly into the life of others.

At the Apollon Theatre an extraordinary representation was advertised. I went there. The building was crowded, glittering with lights, diamonds, and naked shoulders. At first my head reeled with the noisy throng. Where was I? Who were all these people? They had the effect of automatons.

I walked about in the corridor until the curtain rose. I met two students of L'École, who addressed me. I looked at them with astonishment; I did not understand what they were saying. They seemed made of wood; I wanted to satisfy myself by tapping them on the head. I left them in order not to yield to this folly.

I took my seat, near the orchestra. At the first notes of the adorable overture of *La Somnambule* I wanted to cry out, then to take off my clothes, throw them away, and dance obscene dances, naked in the midst of that audience. What had happened to me? I heard my blood ring in my ears, as if a torrent roared through my head. I ground my teeth and clenched my fists, using all the will power that remained to restrain myself, and retain my reason.

Just in front were seated a young man and woman, conversing in hushed voices, and smiling at each other as two lovers might smile, when hearing this music, so full of love. I did not take my eyes from them.

"I am going to kill that man," I muttered. I felt within me a tempestuous rage against this innocent and unconscious lover. What right had he to be happy?

My neighbor on the right kept time to the music with his head, my neighbor on the left reviewed the house with his opera glass. I wanted to speak to one of them, hoping by so doing I might recover my equanimity. I was upon the point of asking them to watch me; but such an effort of reason would have disclosed my insanity.

"I must kill that man."

What will become of me? The crescendo of the orchestra exasperated me. With a determined movement I rose, and in a choking voice, trembling lest I should say too much, I murmured, "Pardon, monsieur."

I passed out, saying to myself:

"If I can only reach the door safely."

I walked on, not daring to look into any of those faces which turned to see who was disturbing so many people; I feared that I should make grimaces at them or insult them.

At last I reached the open air; I inhaled it with long breaths and returned home keeping close to the walls, now and then leaning against them to prevent myself from falling. When in my room, I began beating my head, so besieged was I with thoughts beyond my control, and, beseeching God, I cried out:

"Have mercy, I have done nothing to merit such punishment."

I lay upon the floor till daylight, and awoke shivering with fever; what if I should be sick in my solitude? I had never lived alone, but always with some one who loved me. Was my sickness physical? Did these strange symptoms indicate the Roman fever, a disease so dreaded by strangers?

I called a physician. He felt my pulse, which was abnormally strong, but no sign of malady. He examined my tongue, my gums, put his ear to my heart, my lungs. He questioned me as to my habits. I told him how I had been bred, how I had lived, that my coming to Rome was in consequence of a great sorrow which had completely changed my life. He prescribed long walks, regular work, light nourishment, diversion, and, occasionally, a woman, but solely in a hygienic way, avoiding love. He explained to me the conditions of health, which required an equilibrium between the functions and the faculties. For several years I had indulged in certain habits, that from some cause or other had been interrupted, and I must gradually resume them, somewhat modified, of course, as my conditions were changed, but the physical laws remained unaltered, and I could not hope to violate them with impunity. Just now, he added, I was experiencing the effects of a sirocco, which was unusually severe, and as soon as the wind changed and blew from the mountains, I would feel much better. In short, he advised me to be patient, not to brood, to take care of myself, and above all to seek amusement.

XXIX

The visit and advice of the physician did not improve my condition. He had hardly left me when I received the following letter from M. Ritz:

My Dear Boy

"I write you in the performance of two very pleasant commissions. Several of my colleagues have proposed you for the Academy of Art, and it is but justice. You are beloved, esteemed, and we would extend to you, more especially under the present circumstances, a public testimony of our sympathy. I need not tell you, my young master, how happy it would make me to see you taking the place of our deceased member, you who are so competent to fill the places of the majority of the living members, commencing with myself. This communication is unofficial; but let me have your reply, that you accept with pleasure, and I will attend to all the rest. If agreeable, hold yourself in readiness to return. You know one house where there will be a festival on your arrival. One thing more.

"I have been approached on behalf of a foreigner, desiring to learn whether the original of La Buveuse really exists in marble, and if you would consent to sell it. I am offered forty thousand francs—a handsome price. I believe, however, that I can get fifty thousand. It is a master-piece; but fifty thousand francs for a block of marble, when one has a child, is not to be despised. If you approve, send me an order upon which I can take the statue from your house. I love and embrace you. My son-in-law and my daughter send their regards. Constantin is absent on duty, will soon return."

In big scrawling letters:
"I kiss my dear father.

Felix

Academic ambition was indeed far from my thoughts. My kingdom was no longer of this world, therefore I refused. The sale of La Buveuse, however, I sanctioned. That would be fifty thousand francs more for

Felix; and, since a good man like M. Ritz approved the selling of that souvenir, I could make no objections.

I wrote my master a long letter, and opened my heart. I had nothing to conceal from my only friend, and I felt the need of pouring forth my feelings to some one who loved me. I told him about the resolution I had taken, of the necessity, as it seemed, for me to take my life. I expanded on the worthlessness of everything human and divine in the presence of certain misfortunes; I denied providence. I recalled the names of all those who had suffered unjustly; from this I drew up a charge against Heaven, and in my excitement I concluded my letter by asking M. Ritz to serve as executor of my will and guardian to my son. In short, I gave him all the instructions that a dying man, not sure of the morrow, would give, without perceiving that such a letter was less in the nature of a confidence, than an appeal, and might be summed up in these words:

"Prevent me from killing myself."

The response came promptly. Here it is. Such letters are preserved.

"I shall not advance any of the useless arguments generally offered in such cases. I shall not tell you that God, having given you life, alone has the right to deprive you of it. I shall not say that suicide is immoral, wicked, foolish, a proof of cowardice, rather than courage, or any of the commonplaces which you already know so well. I will say but one word: Did not your mother suffer all that you have? Yes, surely a hundred times more. Did she kill herself? No. Did she not rear you, notwithstanding poverty, abandonment, shame? Your child who, like yourself, is already deprived of one of its natural protectors, has it not doubly need of you? That is the whole question. You have not the right to die.

"I can replace you in the care of your son, you state in your letter—how do you know? And why should you impose upon me, no kinsman of yours, a burden which you are unwilling to take upon yourself? Of course if you should fall in the struggle for existence, mortally wounded on the common battle field, your child would become mine and I would bring him up to honor his father's memory. But if you desert, if you go over to the enemy, if you prove disloyal, and fight against us, what can I say to him, and what kind of an example will you be for him, when he enters the strife?

"How many times have I heard you accuse and curse him, who had abandoned you, though you still had a mother to lean upon. Are you going to give your son the double right of despising his mother and condemning his father? Why attach so little importance to your child? Why not be with him? He is growing, his intelligence is developing, his heart is opening. Why do you leave for others the joy of his first words, his first smiles? Why not try this natural consolation? Why is it that you, who claim to be borne down by the bad influence of an unknown father, do not arm your son in advance against the maternal influence which you know only too well?

"You suffer, is that a new thing? Are you the first man who has suffered? Does not all humanity suffer? You have been betrayed. Genius and love, these two wings of an archangel, which lift man to the celestial spheres, you have had and lost. How many of your fellow-beings crawled upon the earth, admiring and envying you. Did they kill themselves because they were unable to follow you? If genius has gone, work. If you are no longer an artist, be a workman. Make stair-rails, frescos, groups for the ceiling; but at thirty, robust, honest, and respected, do not desert a world where you have need of others, and where others need you. Suicide! Leave it to ruined gamblers, impotent libertines, and dishonest cashiers.

"As to that God whom you blaspheme and deny because he will not tell you his secret, begin by admiring what he shows you, and you will have no time to seek what is hidden from you. Do not reduce him to the narrow proportions of your happiness or pride. He knows why he creates man, and whither he leads him.

"Religion, which in his name commits injustice, errors, excesses, offers you no consolation nor refuge, it does not satisfy your heart; you cannot believe in the sincerity of priests clothed in satin, gold, and precious stones, borne in palanquins, dwelling in palaces and enjoying, before the very eyes of those to whom they preach abstinence and humility, all the good things of this world, not even excepting love. What is that to you? Though priests, they are none the less human, like ourselves weak and corrupted. Forgive them, for they know not what they do. Separate the Christian idea from the men who make a trade of it, and from the forms and ceremonies which incrust it, see the truth, and humble yourself before it. The omnipresence of God is in it. It is indulgence, it is strength, and stands for morality, for charity, for all that is reasonable, good, and true. It discovered repentance, invented forgiveness, and is imperishable in such a world as ours.

"You do not accept the Mysteries. You do not believe in the Incarnation, nor in the Miracles, nor the Resurrection, nor in the

Virginity of the Mother, nor the Divinity of the Son, nor in any of those fantastic legends which follow the life of Jesus upon the earth. Neither do I, but I look upon all these fables as ornaments with which men have clothed the idea to make it attractive and acceptable, in every age, to the imagination, hungering for the supernatural and to whom a religion which appeals to the eyes will ever be preferred to one that merely satisfies the mind.

"And now, my dear boy, if, in spite of all that I have said, you are still unconvinced, and persist in dying, we will mingle our tears with our blame, because we love you with our whole hearts. I shall take care of your child while I live, and after me, my daughter and son-in-law will watch over him, for they are of those who take upon themselves all duties, even those of others. But I ask, or rather I demand, from you one service; for, after all, you are somewhat in my debt for the past, perhaps you owe me something for the future, and you have no right to go off without adjusting our accounts. Make for me in marble, one-third life size, the Moses of Michael Angelo. I have longed all my life to own that master-piece, interpreted by a master. Very little imagination is needed for copying, it will delay you but a short time, and you will not require for that routine work any skill beside that which I have had the good fortune to teach you. It will be but a restitution, and I shall be glad to possess the effort of your chisel. It is important you should gratify me.

"I rely upon you, as you may rely upon me."

XXX

How gently irresistible a philosophy! With what delicacy and admirable shrewdness this generous heart tried to attach me to life by the cords of work, of gratitude, and of dignity.

I replied in these few words:

"I love you with my whole soul. You shall have your Moses. I begin at once."

I had brought to me a reduced copy in plaster of that fine statue and commenced to carve the marble.

After fifteen days of this purely mechanical work which necessitated only experience and precision, I recovered a little of my self-possession. Was I to be cured? Would I be able to forget? What vows I made to God and men, if this miracle should come to pass. When the profile of the grand Hebrew began to emerge from the mass, when the form came out of the block, when the matter took upon it the expression of life, I cried out with joy. Evidently I was saved, provided nothing should again interpose between my art and myself.

I wrote to M. Ritz a letter full of gratitude and enthusiasm. I went in search of those young men whom I had avoided. I visited L'École, where I had not shown myself for several months. I invited two or three to dinner, with excuses for my past neglect. They believed me, or at least pretended to do so. Eight days elapsed.

One morning I received this letter:

"More news; your wife has returned, having discovered some gold mine; that alone can explain her sudden fortune. You remember the splendid mansion erected by Count Attikoff in Cours-la-Reine? Your wife has bought it, with all the furniture and works of art. She paid to the heirs of the count, who died suddenly last month, two millions and a half, and moved into it the day of the sale. She asked the count's servants to remain if they were willing, and they assented, excepting the head coachman, who is English, and would not drive for a single woman without references. It is perfect.

"Your wife has the finest equipage in Paris. She cultivates no society but men, fashionable men, very few and very select. She has her box at the Italiens and at the opera, where she makes a sensation at each representation, for I must tell you, she is more beautiful than ever. She calls herself Madame Iza. The Queen Mother is always with her, adorned with diamonds like a diplomatic snuff box. A coupé of eight springs with the Dobronowska arms awaits them at the door of the theatre; a footman, powdered, with silk stockings, livery bright green, lowers the steps, and a pair of twenty-thousand-franc horses with natural flowers on their head-bands, excite the admiration of the crowd which collects to see the show. From four to six o'clock a drive in the Bois de Boulogne, in an open caleche with four horses. A few calls in their box at the opera, a few visitors at the mansion, but propriety even to virtue. All her old friends are crowded out.

"What is this mystery? Maurice, our stock broker, holds, besides other documents of hers, one certificate of five hundred thousand livres of rente. The day she made the investment, the market advanced three per cent. As to diamonds, rubies, and pearls, she has them as children have marbles.

"Her story as to her fortune is very simple. She 'inherited' several millions. She does not mention the exact sum, nor the name of the testator. But it is generally understood, and it seems to me more probable, that she is protected. By whom? No one has been named, in public at least, but, privately, it is said to be a prince. It is certain that nothing less than royalty could support such luxury away from home.

"Has she found the throne her mother planned for her, second-hand? Rumor has it that he fell in love at first sight, that he was repulsed for a long time, and that, like Jupiter, he must have changed himself into a shower of gold. He is so enamored that he comes here incognito to spend a day or a night. At another time, it is she who disappears for forty-eight hours. She travels alone.

"The servants say nothing, because they know nothing; otherwise, I presume, they would tattle like all domestics. Everybody is puzzled by 'Madame Iza,' and the rich idlers have done their very best to obtain correct information on the subject, without success.

"I thought it my duty to inform you as to what was going on, so that you could decide what course to pursue, should you think of returning to Paris. I am not sorry for this new scandal. It is a positive barrier between that creature and yourself. Until this happened, I was always afraid she would get hold of you again. Now there can be no forgiveness; that would be complicity. She has the good taste or vanity to only use her maiden name, so much the better. The fact that she has been the wife of an honest man, will finally sink into oblivion; and that is the main thing."

To my great astonishment, this unexpected news left me perfectly calm. I laid the letter on my desk and resumed work, determined to think of nothing whatever until I had finished the Moses. I worked until the tools fell from my hands, sleeping only two or three hours, taking them up again as soon as I opened my eyes.

Eight days after this communication I received a second:

"Iza has just written that she must see me, in reference to matters of the highest importance. I am going to her now. Details by next mail.

CONSTANTIN

The next mail brought nothing, nor the second, nor the third, nor the fourth.

The head of Moses was finished.

One morning a letter came, written in an unfamiliar hand. This is what it contained:

"Continue to follow the advice of your good friend Constantin, but you should know that he is your wife's lover."

XXXI

The measure was full.

I called my servant.

A small valise was packed with the indispensables of a hurried traveller. I gave one last look at my marble, which seemed to say to me: "go and return, I will wait you;" and set out for France without any idea of what I should do there, but with the presentiment that I was about to face the gravest event of my whole life. To those about me, I seemed like an automaton. I ate and slept but little and had no clear thought. I was going forward impelled by fate, with the certainty that every step I took led me to something impossible to shun.

I arrived in Paris at six o'clock in the morning, took a bath, changed my clothes, and leaving my valise at the Hôtel de Paris, went direct to Constantin's house.

Seeing me he turned slightly pale, but greeted me cordially. I showed him the anonymous letter.

"It is quite true," he said.

"That you are her lover?"

"For just one hour, the same day I wrote you. God knows I did not intend it, but she did, most decidedly. If she could, by exciting my passion, torture my conscience what a triumph for her after what has passed between us! Nevertheless I have done a mean thing.

"But now I understand, as I could not before, what you have had to suffer. I have felt her power, in spite of all my boasted strength. On leaving her I said to myself: 'You intend to have revenge, serpent; but creatures of your kind cannot capture me. I will see you no more.' The next day I went to her house again. I was not received. She had played me. For three days I was desperately amorous. Ah, if I had been the husband of that woman, and she had gone outside, I—"

He stopped and drew his hand across his forehead.

"What would you have done?" I asked.

"I don't know what I would have done."

"Would you have killed her?"

"I don't say that I would not."

"Then I am stronger than you."

"Perhaps so. Are you embittered against me?"

"No, but I wish you had been frank enough to tell me the truth."

"I did want to go to Rome and relate you all about it, and then—"

"And then?"

"Well—I didn't. What are you going to do in Paris?"

"I am here."

"And that is all?"

"Yes, that is all. Au revoir."

"Where are you bound?"

"My own house first,—afterward, to your father's."

"Shall I see you again?"

"I suppose so," and I left him.

XXXII

I went direct to the Cours-la-Reine, to the well-known residence of Prince Attikoff. I rang and the mansion door opened. I passed through the court, flanked on the right and left with brick stables and carriage houses, with zinc roofs glistening like silver. A bell rang twice to announce the coming of a visitor. Ascending the steps of the entrance which fronted on the quai, I saw through the partially opened door a magnificent lackey in morning livery.

"Madame Iza?" I inquired.

"She is in the country."

"Are you sure of it?"

"Yes, monsieur."

"Since when?"

"Since yesterday."

"When will she return?"

"Today, I believe."

"At what hour can I see her?"

"I don't know, but if monsieur will leave his card, and come again, madame will say if she can see him."

"Very well."

That man doubtless understood from my manner that it was a visit of importance.

I continued:

"Is madame the countess living with her daughter?"

"No, monsieur; she lives near, but she is in the country today with madame."

"Oblige me with writing material, I will leave a note."

I entered the vestibule, a large square room, with mosaic floor, the walls frescoed, like the interiors of Pompeii. In the centre of the vestibule, upon a pedestal, surrounded with aquatic plants and flowers, stood La Buveuse, which Iza had bought under an assumed name, and made the goddess of that temple.

I wrote only these words:

"I will return this evening."

I signed and handed the sealed note to the lackey.

What should I do with myself until evening?

It was then, my friend, that I came to you, to inform you of all that had passed, and to ask you what means of defence the law could give me against such an antagonist. The law could do nothing but separate me from my wife.

Madame Iza would always be Madame Clemenceau. She could always live in the same country in which I lived, dragging my name and that of my son in the mud. Death alone could absolutely separate us. I thank you for the advice which you gave me at that time. You were right, but in my condition reason could do nothing for me. Long hours must pass, before I could seek the presence of Iza. It was the end of April, the anniversary of the happy days of our honeymoon. The places that had witnessed our happiness, what would they say to me, what would they advise; should I interrogate them?

I went out to St. Assise.

I wandered about all day among the well-remembered scenes. I took the little boat which was tied to the bank, and rowed to the willow, underneath which she had sat, the spot where we bathed together I moored the boat to that stump she had grasped so gracefully in emerging from the water. I looked about and listened, my elbows on my knees, my head in my hands. Then I walked in the park, no one seeing me and sat under the pines, half-way up the hill, and reviewed my life.

Who could tell if I should ever again see this place? Where would the morning find me?

The days were still quite short. At seven o'clock it grew dark and I returned to Paris. Two hours later I again presented myself at the palace of the Cours-la-Reine. The same lackey opened one of the side doors of the vestibule. He was now in grand livery, and two others, dressed in the same manner, rose and stood on guard as I passed before them. My guide led me through a series of small rooms hung with satin de chine, brocatelle and lace, warm and sweet with the perfume of flowers, filled with pictures, mirrors, vases, and bronzes, at the farther end of which he opened a door into a boudoir, Louis XVI with panels in white and gold, painted by Fragouard. The curtains, sofas, divans, and chairs were in white satin, embroidered with figures of animals, and demons of every color and form. Turkish carpets, rosewood and lacquer furniture, Sèvres vases, Saxe groups, pendule clocks and chandeliers of Gouttiere, all lit up as if for a banquet.

In the boudoir sat the countess, doubtless anxious to know the object of my visit, before permitting me to see her daughter. To conceal

ALEXANDRE DUMAS, FILS

her embarrassment, although she certainly had had a long experience in ambiguous situations, she was repairing before a mirror a rent in her costume of gray silk trimmed with bows of black velvet; costly rings glittered upon her fingers.

Mothers of this kind are seldom so well caparisoned.

"Good evening, my dear child, how do you do?" said the countess in a parental tone, when the foot man retired, as if she were unaware that anything unusual had occurred between her daughter and myself, or at least anything to be surprised at, or even remembered. The simplicity of the reception bewildered me.

"Thank you, madame, I am very well," I replied, with a bow. There was nothing else to be done.

She continued:

"You called here before?"

"This morning."

"We spent the day in the country, and have only been at home ten minutes. Iza will soon be down, she is changing her dress, she was so covered with dust. There is a dreadful wind blowing this evening. You have just arrived from Rome?"

"Yes, madame."

"It is nearly forty years since I was at Rome, with my father. I was very young then. Shall you remain in Paris permanently?"

"I cannot say, as yet."

"You have done some work in Rome?"

"Very little."

I was about to ask this woman if she were mocking me, when a door opened wide.

"Here is my daughter," said the countess, rising like a lady of honor before a queen.

Iza entered.

I leave you to imagine what passed through my head and heart at this moment.

Iza walked across the room, and saluted me with a little inclination of the head and a faint smile, without speaking. She seemed taller than formerly, perhaps because she stepped with more firmness and authority. She was resplendent in full perfection and bloom. There was a change, however, probably her new manner of life was reflected in her expression. She was more like a portrait of herself, than a living presence. She was not the Iza of the past which I had retained within me. All modesty, even simulated, was forever effaced from that visage, now so bold and assertive.

She was dressed in a simple robe of white taffeta, like the dresses of La République, with wide pleats, short waist, and long skirt, low in the neck. Not a jewel upon her.

The mother and daughter exchanged glances. The mother seemed to ask: "Shall I remain?" The daughter to reply: "It is not necessary."

In fact I was so quiet and self-contained, that neither of these two women could have foreseen, any more than myself, how the interview would end.

"I thank you, mamma," said Iza distinctly, approaching her mother; "good-by till tomorrow."

The countess kissed her daughter's cheek.

"Till tomorrrow," she said.

"We dine together, you remember?"

"Yes, at six o'clock."

"You had better come earlier, I shall not go out."

"I will spend the day, if it is agreeable to you," she continued; and looking toward me, "I am very glad to have seen you again. What a misfortune that you could not have had a better understanding. If you had only listened to me, both of you. And now—"

She extended her hand, which I touched mechanically. I seemed to be in a trance. She went out, and I remained alone with Iza.

XXXIII

S he motioned me to sit down, placing herself opposite, a table between us, and picked up a paper knife, with a jasper handle and vermilion guard, encrusted with garnets, its steel blade inlaid with gold. Was it to keep herself in countenance, or to have a weapon in her hand?

I could not speak. I felt stifled. There was an embarrassing silence. She broke it saying:

"To what am I indebted for this visit, which, I must own, I expected?"

"Expected?"

"Yes."

"For what reason?"

"Because I thought that letter you received at Rome, would bring you."

"It was from you, then?"

"Yes, I wrote it."

"And why?"

"To make you acquainted with your friend, as he had made you acquainted with your wife."

"Then it was true?"

"Does he deny it?"

"No. Why this new infamy?"

"I wished to avenge myself."

"Upon whom?"

"Upon Constantin, who wronged me."

"Was there no other form of vengeance?"

"Yes, but that appeared to me best."

"You are, then, positively a lost woman."

"I am what you made me."

"How so?"

"You should have forgiven me at first."

"Was that possible?"

"You would forgive me today."

"Do you believe that—?"

"I don't believe it, I am sure of it; you love me, and will never love any other woman; if it were false, you would not look as you do, so pale and worn. Why won't you love me as I love you, always?"

"You?"

"Yes, I; there are things that one never forgets."

And she looked me full in the face.

My head began to whirl.

"Why did you deceive me, if you loved me?"

"I don't know; because I was foolish, or because I was bored."

"And those men—?"

"What men?"

"Those to whom you surrendered yourself."

"How can I tell? Did I look at them? What are their names? I don't remember. I was undoubtedly out of my mind, thirsting for some new sensation. But at heart, I loved no one but you. Why did you marry me? I would have been your mistress; you would have loved me, and that would have been all. Did I not propose it? You should have accepted, you, who were so much wiser than I. Where have you been since morning?"

"At St. Assise."

"It must be beautiful there at this season. I have often wished to see that spot again. Suppose we go there together?"

"I should like it very much."

"Truly? Oh, how good you are," said she approaching me. "When? Tomorrow?"

"Yes, but on one condition."

"What is that?"

"That we stay there."

"Forever and ever? That would be a good while. And the winter? And then again, I am not free."

"Wretch!"

I rose toward her with clenched fists. She recoiled, and covering her face with her hands, lowered her head as though expecting a blow:

"If you are going to kill me," said she without changing her attitude, and in a child-like voice, "don't make me suffer."

"Listen to me."

She opened her fingers in front of her eyes and peered through them.

"Speak politely," she replied.

"Are you willing to go away with me?"

"At once?"

"At once."

"No."

"Then there must be an end to it. Do you choose that we die together?"

"What folly, at our age. Why die? We love each other. Look at me: I am beautiful, and you, too, are handsome, when you are not angry. Time enough to die when one is old. Why do you make a scene? Could we live together, after all that has passed? That would be base, you would be laughed at: I would not like that, for I know you are the best man in the world, as you are one of the greatest artists; thank me a little for that. Do you know that I had but one wish? To possess La Buveuse. You have seen it again; what a masterpiece!

"Let us leave things as they are. I require luxury, excitement, folly. Leave me in my natural element, and only take from me what I can give you. We are not congenial. You are a child; I am a bad woman; but I love you, and I would like to have you again. I know you thoroughly, and I am sure that you have been faithful, even while hating me. If you knew how happy I am when I think of that; it is so good to own somebody exclusively. Take your choice. You belong to me. I am a courtesan, a vile and despicable creature, it is true, but you love me. It is your destiny, accept it. I will tell you what we will do. You remain at Paris; you must remain, you must make more beautiful things, I wish it. Nobody will know that you have seen me, you will never speak of me, or when you do, say that I am a wretch. It is all the same to me. Do you wish a public scandal? Do you want to go to law? The law will separate us, for we are not yet separated. You could compel me to return if you chose. That is not what you want? You will go back alone, not just now;" she continued, putting her arms around my neck; "and any time when you want to see me, you have only to write this one word: 'come,' and I will fly to you with a veil over my face as when I came from Warsaw; do you remember? No one will know it is I, and for a day, for a night, for a minute, just as you like, I will be yours, entirely yours, yours alone, your Iza as before, your plaything; will you?"

"In other words, my wife would be my mistress?"

"Words don't signify anything."

"And when shall we begin the new life?"

"Whenever you choose."

"Immediately."

She hesitated a moment.

"Suppose the prince should come," said I, as if agreeing to this strange proposition.

"So they have told you, have they? Oh, there is no danger, and anyhow it doesn't matter, now I am rich. Wait a moment. I will send away everybody, but you will have to leave before daylight. Stay here till I call you."

And I felt her hot lips on mine, lips belonging to a body without a soul.

"I adore you," she whispered, and disappeared.

Not a word about her son.

I remained there several minutes stupefied, then I heard this single word, passing like a breath:

"Come."

I entered that infamous gynecium, a den padded with wadding and satin, to muffle the cries of love. A soft, pale light, like winter moonbeams, fell from the transparent ceiling, revealing a voluptuous form with arms extended toward me.

What a mistress, what science, what a picture of pleasure.

A courtesan to infatuate a king.

And only twenty-three.

At one o'clock in the morning she slept, calm as a virgin.

If this creature should live another day, she would make me the most despicable of men.

XXXIV

I arose and went into the boudoir for the knife with which she had been playing two hours before; then I returned to the bed chamber and lay down beside her. Her breathing was gentle and regular. She smiled. Never had she been so beautiful.

Two o'clock struck.

I touched her lightly on the shoulder. Her lips moved instinctively as if expecting a kiss.

"Do you love me," I asked.

"Yes," she murmured, dreamily.

It was her last word. I wanted it to be the last she should pronounce in this world. I pressed my left hand upon her forehead, throwing her head backward, and with all the strength of my right, plunged the knife into her bosom just below the left breast. She started up under the force of the thrust, and with one sigh, fell back on her pillow. I sprang from the bed and listened.

She ceased to breathe. A few drops of blood trickled from the wound.

I LEFT THE HOUSE, WANDERED about the streets till morning, and at the dawn of day, gave myself up, a prisoner.

THE END

A Note About the Author

Alexandre Dumas, fils (1824–1895) was a French novelist and playwright. Named after his father, the famed author of such novels as *The Count of Monte Cristo* (1844) and *The Three Musketeers* (1844), he was raised in Paris and educated from a young age. In 1831, Dumas, fils—an illegitimate child—was recognized by his father, who eventually took him away from his mother, a dressmaker. After years in various boarding schools, Dumas, fils moved to his father's home in Saint-Germain-en-Laye in 1844 and embarked on a career as a professional writer. As the grandson of Thomas-Alexandre Dumas, a decorated general of Revolutionary France whose mother was an African slave, Dumas, fils was greatly inspired by his family history. His first major success came with the romantic novel *The Lady of the Camellias* (1848), which he adapted into a popular play that would inspire Verdi's opera *La Traviata* (1853). Inspired by the reception of this work, he committed himself to the theater and largely abandoned novel writing. A notable outlier of this turn of events is *The Clemenceau Case* (1866), a successful semi-autobiographical work. In 1894, Dumas, fils, a member of the Académie française for twenty years, was appointed to the prestigious *Légion d'honneur* for his contribution to French literature.

A Note from the Publisher

Spanning many genres, from non-fiction essays to literature classics to children's books and lyric poetry, Mint Edition books showcase the master works of our time in a modern new package. The text is freshly typeset, is clean and easy to read, and features a new note about the author in each volume. Many books also include exclusive new introductory material. Every book boasts a striking new cover, which makes it as appropriate for collecting as it is for gift giving. Mint Edition books are only printed when a reader orders them, so natural resources are not wasted. We're proud that our books are never manufactured in excess and exist only in the exact quantity they need to be read and enjoyed.

Discover more of your favorite classics with Bookfinity™.

- Track your reading with custom book lists.
- Get great book recommendations for your personalized Reader Type.
- Add reviews for your favorite books.
- AND MUCH MORE!

Visit **bookfinity.com** and take the fun Reader Type quiz to get started.

Enjoy our classic and modern companion pairings!

Printed in the USA
CPSIA information can be obtained
at www.ICGtesting.com
JSHW082350140824
68134JS00020B/2001

9 781513 291321